Sun-Daughters, Sea-Daughters

SUN-DAUGHTERS, SEA-DAUGHTERS

AIMEE OGDEN

A TOM DOHERTY ASSOCIATES BOOK

NEW YORK

This is a work of fiction. All of the characters, organizations, and events portrayed in this novella are either products of the author's imagination or are used fictitiously.

SUN-DAUGHTERS, SEA-DAUGHTERS

Cover art by Chase Stone
Cover design by Christine Foltzer

Edited by Christie Yant

A Tordotcom Book
Published by Tom Doherty Associates
120 Broadway
New York, NY 10271

www.tor.com

Tor® is a registered trademark of
Macmillan Publishing Group, LLC.

ISBN 978-1-250-78213-7 (ebook)
ISBN 978-1-250-78212-0 (trade paperback)

First Edition: February 2021

For my daughter, for my son: I dreamed of you, too.

Sun-Daughters, Sea-Daughters

Atuale leaves without saying goodbye.

Saareval sleeps with his eyes half-closed. She lays a hand lightly on his chest, one more time, to gauge its hitching rise and fall. No better than the day before; no worse either. When she lifts her hand, two of his scales come away clinging to her palm. They fall onto the tectonic ridges of the bedsheet, gray at the growth edge and angry red in the middle—so very different from the cool clay color of her own. She scrapes them into a tiny glass vial and adds it to the pouch strapped around her waist, where it clinks hopefully against more like it: miniature amphorae of blood and lymph.

She closes her hand into a fist to keep herself from reaching out to touch his face. She longs to wake him, and dares not. He would not stop her from what she plans to do—could not, in the ashes of this all-consuming fever. But if he should open his eyes now, and only look at her with the fear that he might die without her to soothe his slide beneath those forever-waves . . . Atuale is a strong woman, but strength is no barrier to a bone-knife of guilty grief slipped beneath the breastbone. "Teluu is gone," she whispers, too softly to wake him. The others will let him know, if he swims up to lucidity later today. Telling him herself is the threadbare excuse she dressed herself in to justify lingering for a last moment here beside him.

Teluu was the first of the household to take ill. Ten days, scarcely a moment more, and then gone. So fast, so quiet, as if she hadn't wished to burden the sisterhouse any longer. Saareval is younger than her, stronger too, one of the last to take ill. How long can he hold out, before this fever drags him under its dark surface too? None of the Vo are young enough, strong enough, to fight the plague forever.

It is not youth or strength that has protected Atuale from illness.

She slips out of their pairdwelling and through his family's sisterhouse unnoticed, though the sun casts long shadows through the open windows. Most of his siblings and cousins have taken with the fever now too. Unlike Saareval, they might have tried to stop her, but they lie upon their own sickbeds. Atuale wraps her arm protectively around the case at her waist anyway. A few still-healthy cousins, exhausted from caring for the afflicted, do not stir from their sleep in the common room and the courtyard as Atuale ghosts by on bare, silent feet. Toward a livable future. Toward the bleached-coral bones of her past.

The plague-stricken town is as silent as the sister-house. Not even the tallgrass hung in open windows rustles, for want of wind. A greasy miasma of illness clings to the air, and Atuale takes short, shallow breaths. She walks from the tightly packed sisterhouses of the town center to where the buildings spread farther out from one another and lean gardens can sprawl between one door and the next. Until finally the whole town is at her back and she stands at the top of the cliff-stairs.

At the bottom, dizzyingly far below, the sea hammers the shore. That stone landing seems a galaxy and more away. Atuale starts walking anyway. At first she tries counting the steps, to numb the pain of the worry that presses behind her eyes. But she loses count time and again. Little clothing drapes her, in the Vo way: only a wide sash that covers her genitals and a shawl to shade her smooth-scaled head and shoulders. Enough protection from the heat for the high-ceilinged sisterhouses, but out here the sun pours its warmth into each and every scale. The steps she takes downward sap the strength from her legs but don't seem to bring her any closer to sea level—only farther from Saareval.

Halfway down, she slips on an eroded step and tumbles down three more. Tears clot her vision as she rubs her bruised knees. She picks over her legs, looking for cuts. Looking for infected, color-bled scales. There are none, of course. Guilt flushes her chest, only to be scrubbed quickly away by determination and relief.

Water from her tin cools the parched salt-tang in her throat and she lies back against the steps, her ribs scraping the stone with each shuddering breath. Halfway down, but the towering cliff has already long since cut her off from any last sights of the silica-sparkling roofs of Keita Vo; even the Observatory has fallen behind the craggy wall. Atuale turns her face away from the empty, stone-split sky.

Below there is only open ocean for as far as she can see. And on such a cloudless, flung-open day as this one, she can see very far indeed. Atuale balances between two lives, this one and the last, and finds the position more precarious than she would have liked.

She pushes herself up to a sit, then a stand. Her knees and ankles ache; her shoulders too. This is a small price to pay. She would climb down a staircase as wide as the world is round, if it meant saving Saareval's life. She would walk the whole way on the points of knives. There will be time to rest when she has secured his safety. Perhaps if she is pleasant, if she remembers the silver-smooth tongue of the Greatclan Lord's daughter that once she spoke so fluently, she may be able to negotiate a morsel of food, a brief rest of her weary legs before she mounts the cliff-stairs again.

Or perhaps it would be best to be home sooner. Her throat tightens against tears she has no time to shed. Instead she lets her head fall forward under its own weight to stare down at the green-touched waves that break below. If she leaned forward just a little farther, she would fall.

She does not think the sea would welcome her return.

Instead she frowns very hard at the horizon, toward the north. She thinks she can see the Khelesh station just there, the tip of the great turret gun disrupting the smooth curve of the world. Pointed upward: a reminder from the Greatclan Lord to the land-dwellers of Keita Vo of the power and presence of the undersea kingdom. A second turret gun is barely visible, a twisted hulk that mostly sleeps beneath the surface now. Atuale remembers singing the blessing-song for its commission. She remembers her father, the Greatclan Lord, smearing his blood on the steelica base to infuse it with his own strength and power. A waste of time, that he should grandstand for the benefit of the quiet, insular Vo. He has struggled enough over the past twenty years to cling to his own tattered collection of clans. But then, the Greatclan Lord has always prized appearance over actuality.

Breath comes almost evenly now. Her legs have stopped shaking, too—or at least she must pretend that it is so. She puts one hand on her belly and pulls in a rib-scraping breath, and she struggles back up to her feet. It was easier passing upward, all those years ago. But she was younger then, and she wasn't bearing the burden of a return voyage. She sets her foot on the next stone down, and the one after that. Each one is like a step backward in time, toward when she was young and naïve, with scarcely an adult's worth of fatpads to guard her against the worst of the winter's currents. Age does not fall away from her as she moves downward, though, and her feet and knees continue to throb as she draws closer and closer to the surface of the water, to the seaclans she once belonged to. Her scales cling fast. Her throat does not split open to reveal long-shuttered gills. Gene-eater technology is stronger than the pull of the past.

Saareval, her footfalls whisper against the rock. Her heart thunders a matching rhythm. *Saareval, Saareval.* Perhaps he will thank her for these efforts on his behalf. Perhaps he will not. She didn't stop to ask his opinion one way or the other. It's all right if he decides to hate her, afterward. One has to be alive, to hate.

At low tide, the World-Witch's house peeks through the shifting waters that slash at the steep cliffs: three pearl-glass domes, bubbling up from the bottom of the shallow sea. Since Atuale was a girl—since they both were, she and the Witch together—the World-Witch has conjured technological trinkets and toys from across the scattered humanholds of the universe. Do you need nanofilters to scrub Vo mining runoff from the precious water where your children are crèched? The Witch can magic some up. Do you desire to break your heart upon the newest Keilishk songpearls? You need only ask the Witch.

Do you want gene-eaters to reshape yourself, body and soul, to mold you for life on land instead of water? The Witch, of course, can arrange such a thing. For a price.

When the cliffside path brings Atuale near enough to spot them, the reflection off the curved surfaces prevents her from seeing whether the Witch is at home. If she isn't, if this has been for nothing— Atuale severs the strand of this possibility before it can tie knots in her heart. The Witch *must* be there, and so, she will be.

But here is a new worry to catch Atuale in its nets, as she draws closer to the bottom of the path: she doesn't know how to get inside.

There will be a sea-door, and she can guess at where it should lie. She has never been to this place of the Witch's; they knew each other before, in the court of the Great-clan Lord. Before the Witch was a Witch, before she was anything but Atuale's dearest companion, Yanja. But sea-door or not, Atuale isn't sure she should dare an underwater search. She has made herself a creature of earth and air, no longer a child of the water. The sea is no more forgiving a parent than Atuale's father ever was.

The tide is drawing in, and by the time Atuale reaches the smooth-swept landing at the bottom of the stairs, she can see nothing but the clear, empty pearlglass at the top of the domes. "Hello!" she cries, as if the Witch inside could hear her over the bellow of the waves. She throws a pebble at the dome, which glances off unanswered. She sits down and crosses her legs into a breathing-prayer pose, numbers the gods, and begs each one for a moment's mercy. When she stands again, her legs are tingling. The dome remains still and silent.

She paces the landing, and wonders why she never interrogated this moment, this arrival, in her heart until now. Because her heart has been overfull of other worries, perhaps. Because she has been occupied with the ending of this story rather than its beginning.

Or because she is in some ways still the same foolish, headstrong child as ever, and that child never had to wonder how to enter a sea-dwelling with land-scaled skin and sealed-up gills.

The sea grows stormcloud-dark with evening's approach, and its spray dances tauntingly around her ankles. Her belly churns nauseously to match the push and pull of the waves. She walks to the edge, turns, and presses all the way back to touch the cliff face. Her shoulders are as strong as they ever were, though her legs are wearied from the day's exertion. She cups her hands, turns them back and forth to look them over; she flexes her feet.

Impossible to forget a birthright, however long you turn your back to it.

She offers the sea-wind her sash and shawl and it tears them away from her, as if denying her the right to change her mind now. Without the cushion of her clothes, she cinches her case of precious samples tighter about her waist. She licks her lips and tastes salt. She could change her mind anyway, walk back up naked and exposed to burning sunlight and blasting wind.

Her hand leaves the cliff. She runs lightly over the wet rock and leaps out as far as she can toward the domes. Cold water slams over her head before she remembers to steal one last breath from the air.

She never had to do that, before.

Salt stings her eyes when she forces them open underwater. With both arms she reaches and pulls. Somewhere, somewhere beneath the Witch's home there has to be a waterlock. She only has to find it—

Her own weight pulls her downward, parallel to the dome but not toward it. She was never so *dense* before.

Light shatters on the dome's surface and these sharp splinters pierce her vision as it goes black about the edges. Her arms, pulling upward, pulling forward, are strong. But the ocean is stronger.

So Saareval will die, after all. So Atuale will, too. Her one regret, now, is that they did not die together. But they never would have, would they? They have spent twenty years lining up the ragged edges of their differences and never yet found a match but one. But one, and that one is love, and Atuale clings to it as the ocean drinks her down into its darkness.

———————

Atuale wakes to faint, pulsating light on her face. More important, Atuale *wakes*.

She sits up and kicks off the knit blanket that covers her legs; the bristly hairs that poke up between her scales snag it in several places before she gets it free. Her hand gropes at her waist—there is nothing there. The samples! They'll be at the bottom of the sea now, and with them, her hopes for Saareval. She chokes on a sob, and lurches upright.

When her feet strike the floor beside the couch, the floor squelches under her weight. "Where am I?" she rasps, the words catching in her ragged throat. But she already knows, from the wave-washed glass dome over-head, from the sweet and sickly smells that percolate up through her awareness. It seems the Witch has rescued her from another predicament. Atuale changes tack. "Where are *you*?"

A shadow moves in her periphery. Atuale spins, but the tall figure lounging at the opening to the adjacent dome isn't her Witch. "I think this is yours," he says, and tosses her something.

She recognizes the squarish shape too late. "Be careful!" she gasps, but she catches the sample case and clutches it to her chest. It's damp, but when she examines it with shaking hands, the inside remains dry, the glass vials secure.

She looks up at the stranger as she secures the case back around her hips. "Thank you." The tightness in her shoulders slackens as she scans his face. She doesn't recognize him, though his pale, faintly mottled gray coloration matches the Witch's—he might share the same low-caste homeclan. A half-sibling, or cousin? His face is painted like hers always was, too, with purpled streaks of grease-dye to highlight cheekbones and brow.

"Looking for a clan tattoo?" he drawls. He's speaking the local Vo dialect, not any seaclan language, for her benefit. He shifts his hip to show off just such a mark: it is indeed the stylized net of the Mzo Ma, the northern

farmers and fisherfolk. The Witch's people. The movement also brings into the light the lines of his penis-slit;
too late, Atuale remembers to be embarrassed of their
mutual nudity. She snatches the blanket, knots it loosely
around her waist out of defiance more than anything else.
She is still more seaclan than she would like to admit,
even to herself, let alone this interloper in her story.

Atuale lifts her chin. "I came looking for the World-
Witch."

The stranger clucks. "Atuale, I'm disappointed. Of
course it's been a long time, but you mustn't be so for-
mal." His lips pull into a sideways smile. "Aren't we
friends, even after all that's passed? You really should use
my clan-name."

A frown tugs at Atuale as she looks at the stranger
again, searching for familiarity in the hard, lean lines of
face and body. He's older than her, though not by much,
and though he wears the mark of the Mzo Ma, his hands
don't show the strength or the wear of that wearying
work. When she peers closely at the short fur on his
flanks, she can see the faded gravid-spots underneath.
He's borne young, a long time ago. She looks back at his
face and she can see now a familiar ghost overlaid on the
thin lines of his face; she sees where the skin lies oddly
over hips that once carried generous fatpads.

"It's you," she says, and this time her voice cracks. Her

confidante, savior, pillow-friend, betrayer. Her quest has been successful, and yet she finds herself taken aback. Saareval and his kin trade often with the World-Witch, yet he has never mentioned this development to Atuale. Her shoulders hunch. Of course Saareval speaks little of the World-Witch despite his dealings. She's made no secret of avoiding the Witch's shuttlecraft on the occasions it lands in the Vo village. "You changed," she says, rather stupidly.

The World-Witch—*Yanja*, then, if he's going to insist on informality—smiles. "Not unexpectedly. It's an isolated life I lead, and in the absence of a male . . ." The gill slits in his throat flare briefly, matching the grin on his face. "Well, the usual thing happened."

Atuale's hand sweeps through a broad gesture, taking in her own scaled body, webless hands and feet, and sealed-over gill slits. "Your otherworld gene-eaters made me this. If you wanted to avoid the Change, you could have easily enough." *It suits you,* she doesn't quite manage to say. *You look well. You look happy.* There's a twenty-year-old weight in her throat that blocks the words. Atuale was young and stupid then, had no thought except for what she wanted—or did not. Yanja was young then too, but not stupid. Never stupid. Atuale got what she wanted, but Yanja did too. And what Yanja had wanted was blood.

"Enjoying the view?" Yanja says, and smiles. His teeth

are as sharp as ever, though yellowed with time's passage. "Or looking in the mirror of might-have-been? I don't remember that you ever thanked me."

"You want thanks?" There's real anger behind those words. She thought she had put aside her hurt here, but it seems she has only painted over it. When she takes a deep breath to steady herself, the humid air rattles in her clamped throat. "I thought you helped me then because—" Her throat jerks. "Because we were friends."

"Were!" Yanja exclaims. "Are we no longer? You wound me."

"Making me Vo started a clan war."

"Stopping you from *changing* started a clan war." Yanja shrugs. "It's not my fault that your darling father promised a prince to the Prequ clan." He saunters into the room and drops onto the couch Atuale has just gotten up from. Fight or flight, her tremulous pulse insists; her heart tears the possibility of flight away and shreds it into a thousand pieces. She wants more than to fight. She wants to hurt him. She wants to hurt him back. "Mind you, he wouldn't have stayed any fonder of you if you'd gone Vo after you'd spawned a few brats on the Prequ first."

Atuale's claws press into her own thighs. She needs him. Saareval needs him. She can't hurt him, so she hurts herself. Through those ten tiny points of pressure, the viciousness drains out of her words, leaves them empty. "The Mzo Ma are free of the Greatclan Lord's holdings. I'm glad for you. For them. But the Greatclan and the Prequ are still shedding blood over that broken promise." So *many* promises were broken when Atuale went to the land. She hates herself for even being angry. Hadn't she and Yanja so often spoken, hadn't they wept, over the abasement of the lowclans? She would have helped them if she could. She would have sworn herself to Yanja's plan.

If she had known it. If she hadn't been just a Greatclan princess to be used up and cast aside by a Witch on his way to his own better world.

She makes herself take a long, deep breath. She makes herself think of Saareval, and of calm. The two walk ever hand in hand, for her. "Your people have their independence. The Greatclan is no longer great. Do you still need my thanks, with all that accounted between us?"

"It's a start." Yanja smiles. "So what is it that brings you back to me, after all this time? And all that dreadful bloodshed?" He flings one arm up over his eyes, and peers at her from beneath the bend of his elbow. "Your father still lives, by the way. Is that a relief or a burden?"

"I know." The seas give off rumor and gossip like they give off mist. The Lord of the Greatclan still rules, the last she has heard. Though of course his holdings in the northern and western clans have been greatly reduced since Atuale's time. And his dignity, as well. Atuale's lips thin in something between a smile and a frown. She turns away from Yanja's smug invitation to anger, picking her way over the soft mossy floor. "We aren't completely cut off from clan news up there. The lowclans still take our trade, and the western ones sometimes too."

"We! Our! So you really have gone native." Yanja rolls over onto his belly for a closer look at her. "How are the mods working out for you? It looks itchy, having your old fur poking out all hither and thither and yon. It's not itchy, is it?" He doesn't wait for an answer. "I certainly hope your mods aren't starting to break down after all this time. Not least because the gene-eaters are long since out of warranty, and I don't imagine you could afford a new installation." His enduring smile sharpens. "You couldn't even afford it the first time around."

Atuale stops beside a driftwood table. It takes her weight when she leans on it with both hands. "I thought you were helping me out of kindness. Out of friendship." Yanja wasn't her only pillow-friend, of course; all the mateless girls in their cohort took turns with one an-other, teaching each other how to enjoy their bodies in between the loveless ministrations from the young males of other clans. But it was special, the time she had with Yanja, their quiet hours together, when Atuale could es-cape her father's shadow for a spell, could intoxicate herself on otherworld wines and Yanja's body. Her dry tongue scrapes the roof of her mouth. She hates her old self, and loves her too, soft and far-dreaming thing that she was. "I thought—"

"I'm sure you thought a lot of things." She can't see his face now, but she can still hear that smile. "Not new mods, then. What, then—has the shine started to wear off with what's-his-scales? Do you need some attraction pheromones? Does he? Or maybe something for your darling in-laws to finally welcome you into the clan? A little oxytocin hybrid vapor, perhaps, to induce that desperately needed family bonding? Or—oh! A mouthwash to take the edge off that egg-eater breath?"

"I came because of the plague," Atuale snarls. The curl of her claws leaves shallow scores on the tabletop. "You know that."

Yanja clucks. "There's knowing, and there's *knowing*. He's got it then too, your little lordling?"

"We don't have lords. It's not like the clans up there." Atuale bites her tongue against more. Yanja knows all this, too. "They need your help."

"Then *they* should ask me." On that, Yanja's voice flattens. Atuale turns and finds him sitting up now, elbows on knees. His silver-dark eyes are on her. He's from the lowclans, who have always been the turret fodder for sea-clan skirmishes against the Vo rather than the instigators, but there's no reason to expect Yanja wastes much love on the Vo. Isolated up on their mountain by will as much as by geography, the Vo do not constrain themselves with obligation. Loyalty and duty bind together family and community, never outsiders. *We make our own way,* the Vo tell themselves. Yanja's services are dear and the Vo seek out the Witch only when they muster enough money to buy a single shipment of precious off-world steelica or seeds.

Atuale, however, will gladly tie whatever chains of debt she must around her neck. Yet another reason to suspect she is not truly Vo at her heart and never will be.

Yanja smiles sharply, as if he can read her thoughts. "*They* should do a lot of things. Shouldn't they? But *you're* here."

She will not be made to feel a foolish child again. She squares her shoulders, raises her chin. "I need your help, Yanja. The Vo need a cure and you can bring it to them. Ask your price. And don't tell me this time you'll do it out of the kindness of your heart, because I know that you haven't got any."

"No kindness? Or no heart?" Yanja drawls. "Now, Atuale. If you're so desperate for help, why not go to the other side of the island and find Star-Hunter? Or the Greatleap Marcher? It's not really me you need. Is it?"

Because they cut corners and skirt the edges of interstellar law, but Yanja's reputation is unscratched by unlicensed contraband and legal red tape. "I'm here," she says simply.

Yanja's face relaxes. "All right. Lord or not, I know our dear Saareval is contract-maker for Keita Vo."

Atuale's back-scales bristle at the words *our dear Saareval* on Yanja's lips. "He's on the committee."

"He *runs* the committee. Titles don't make the man, my coral." Yanja's tongue flicks behind his teeth, caged behind a hungry grin. "I want an exclusive contract. I can get building materials from off-world cheaper than the Naraqui can offer, or the Haabian Vo either, even with the cost of fuel factored in. Or make me a middleman on the existing deals, I don't really care which; I'll see to it my cut comes out the same."

"You know I can't promise anything in his name."

He stands and crosses the distance between them. "There's knowing," he says. He's taller than her now, or was he always? Memory breaks and blurs. "And then there's *knowing*."

She holds his gaze as long as she can, then jerks away. "Fine. If a little ill-earned coin is the best you can dream of? It's yours." She bites off a *What else?* No need to give Yanja an opening; he will take one or make one as he wishes.

"Typically I require something a little more solid than

dreams. Coin will do nicely, thank you."

"You could have asked me for coin the last time. Instead you took blood. Without asking." Not Atuale's blood, either. That, she might have known how to forgive.

"There's one more thing, too. A personal favor, let's call it." He reaches out to finger the knotted blanket over her hip. Her haunches tighten, but she keeps herself from stepping back. "Looks like you packed lightly for a long trip. Or is your luggage currently being battered into pieces on the rocks?"

"What?" She shakes her head, but it does not clear. "I can't go *with* you." She already has one otherworld, that's all she needs. And she has someone waiting who needs her too. But dizzying images of far-off suns dance across her vision, the spices and songs of otherworlds she has only dreamed of.

"A seal-eyed, earnest, just-about-widow? You'll knock *at least* twenty-five percent off the asking price of any antiphage. This isn't a request, by the way; it's a condition. My world's not any worse without the Vo in it."

Saareval needs her. But a cure is what he needs most of all. She can bring that to him, and nearly convince herself it is only for him that she does it. Atuale left the sea to kiss the mountains and the sky. Of course she wants to embrace the stars as well. Desire steals the air from her lungs, suffocating the only answer. She nods instead.

He smiles and moves past her; his shoulder bumps her on the way by. "I need to get my ship ready. You've got two hours, give or take; make yourself at home and try not to break anything."

She slides into the chair beside the driftwood table and stares at her open palms.

It was never really a decision at all.

―――――――

Atuale can't possibly remember the moment she was spawned, but she does anyway.

Or perhaps she only feels like she remembers it, and isn't that how brains work anyway, what you believe you remember is just as real as what you truly do?

She drifts. Galaxies of bubbles swirl over her head, borne upward on warmer currents. Light splinters on dissolved particulates with the wisdom of a thousand ancient suns. Her mother's nearness, pulsating close and warm. Dark nebulae of blood and birth-fluid embrace one another in knots and clots. Atuale was born here. She needs to go back.

In dreams, she thinks she remembers her mother's name, too, even her clan, but when she wakes these false memories dissolve. The only lingering reality is that moment of imprinting, the time and place where she was born, where she must give birth. And the knowledge that slices that truth to ribbons is this: she has never found her way back to that moment, and, it seems with each passing year, she never will.

———————

Atuale's world shudders and shifts. She startles awake, bolting upright, and finds herself slouched in the chair beside Yanja's table. This time, it doesn't take her as long to orient herself in this upside-down world with its ocean for sky.

Opposite her, Yanja has his hip up against the table. Now he gives it another jolt for good measure. "Plenty of time to sleep between jumpweb gates," he scolds. He's put on clothes, from neck to toe, some kind of thick and form-fitting garment. In his hand he holds a folded-over lump of fabric, which he presses into her hands as she staggers up. "Here. Get dressed. You're not exactly built for warmth anymore."

The cloth feels strange when she slides her hands over it, almost rubbery, not at all like the soft and lightweight fabrics she's grown accustomed to wearing on land. It's not the harsh light of the sun she'll need protection from out there. She hurries to put it on, cramming one leg and then the other awkwardly into the tight-fitting tubes of the legs, her arms into the sleeves. Ridges and valleys of cloth stack up at her elbows and ankles; the suit is clearly meant for someone taller and broader in the shoulders. It's functional, at least—she already feels overwarm in the humid pearlglass dome.

"Come on, then." Yanja jerks his head to the left. She scowls at his back as she follows him through the tunnel into the secondary dome. On the other side, she has to crawl through the open jaws of a rust-chewed waterlock to emerge into what must be Yanja's hangar. She's never been in here before, though she's seen his ship arc through the air over Keita Vo now and again. Somehow it seems smaller up close, sleeping atop its platform. A knot of algae drifts through the water above the dome, playing shadows over the little vessel's steelica hull. It doesn't matter how big the ship is. It carries hope for Saareval, for all the Vo.

Whether they want it or not. Atuale sets her jaw, and helps Yanja start carrying packages of food and supplies up through the open hatch into the ship's belly.

Once everything is stowed, Yanja works through a checklist of pre-takeoff tasks. Atuale tries to assist at first, but the consoles are beyond her understanding; the Vo have nothing like this technology and she's out of practice. When she tries to take over reading the list, she struggles to sound out the syllables of cramped, intricate seaclan writing, to make sense of a language she has done her best to forget for twenty years. Finally Yanja dismisses her and takes over both the list and the work himself. "Count bolts or sing a working-song or whatever it is you do for fun up there," he mutters.

Atuale wanders deeper into the ship and finds a loose panel cover to pick at. Being useless hurts. That's why she came to the World-Witch in the first place: because she could not bear to watch her husband die, sitting helplessly and unable to ease his pain as healthy scales peeled away and left oozing pink sores in their wake, as he grew too weak first to cook their evening-meals, then to eat them unaided. And his siblings, his whole damnable clan, sickening alongside him and unwilling to reach out for help. *We make our own way:* the closest thing they have to a religious belief. No gods to pray to, no friends to reach out to. Atuale doesn't know what she believes anymore, but she knows that turning one's back on hope for a cure, while loved ones and elders and children ail and ache and die? With or without gods to weigh in on the matter, that is too great a sin to let stand.

By the time she's tightened the panel up, her longest claw serving as screwdriver, Yanja calls her back up to the front. "Buckle in," he says briskly. "There's no sea too broad to swim, if you start your journey early enough."

Yanja's chair and its harness show signs of long wear and tear: scratched metal, fraying straps, a small explosion of foam from an overworked seam. The twinned seat beside it shows no such overuse. The buckles gleam, the padding is firm when Atuale slides into it. She wonders how often the World-Witch has shown passengers behind the curtain of his work. Has any other flown alongside him to see how, exactly, he bargains for the trinkets and toys and, occasionally, miracles that he brings back from the otherworlds?

"Where will we go?" she asks as he coaxes the ship to light-blinking, gentle-humming life around them. The front-facing window clears with the charge running through it, and sunlight trickles down onto her face. "And how long do you expect it will take?"

"Two days, round trip. Takes a little while longer going than coming back, thanks to jumpweb orientation." Yanja frowns at a panel, taps another. "Think your best-beloved can hold on that long?"

She answers with half her mind, the remainder left accounting Saareval's time. Two days is forever, but she hopes it will be short enough. "The Vo are stronger than you think."

"Egg-eaters," says Yanja, though there's no venom in the word. "Are you buckled in? I'm not stopping mid-flight to nursemaid you if you smash your head open on the glass."

She pulls a face, but Yanja isn't looking at her. She gives

the restraints a grudging tug. They hold firm. "I'm ready when you are."

Yanja presses a button. A deep groan from the dome outside nets Atuale's attention; the metal lock clangs as it clamps shut. Then a cascade thunders down onto the window, and she has to smother a cry: the dome has parted overhead and given way to foaming seawater. At-uale sits up straighter against the seat and does not check Yanja's expression for a reaction. He says only, "It would have been less impressive at low tide."

The engines fire, blasting steam skyward, and the ship breaks free of the water. Atuale cranes forward to watch the surface of the water skim by beneath them. Here and there she thinks she can just make out the dim structures of clanholds before Yanja tugs on the pilot's yoke and turns the nose skyward.

"Fifteen minutes till we break atmosphere." There's something harder underlining his usual drawling disin-terest. Perhaps he's darkly amused that she still carries some awe for the magnificent, ancient clanholds where she grew up. Atuale is what she is, but she also was what she was.

A tinny voice jolts out of the frequency crystal in the ship's console. "Unknown vessel, this is the Greatclan Watch. You will return to sea level immediately. All off-world travel is interdicted by order of the Greatclan Lord."

"And since when must we all dance to his tune?" mutters Yanja, before he tunes the frequency crystal for input. "Greatclan Watch, this is the *Unfortunate Wanderer,* as you know very well." His voice is somehow both loud and languid, a contrived tone that Atuale remembers well from their days in her father's halls. "I have license from six different clans to come and go at my leisure. So, kindly eat my wake."

"Return to sea level immediately or we will fire on you."

Atuale's lungs crush under the double weight of acceleration and alarm. "Yanja," she says, and her sharp teeth slice into her lower lip. The vulnerability of this tiny vessel, and with it her mission, is suddenly overwhelming. She wishes she had the sample case to hold close to her heart, but it is safely stowed in Yanja's radiation-proofed hold. A single kinetic pulse from the Khelesh station turret and this ship will drop out of the sky, never to lift again. Saareval will perish, perhaps his entire people too.

Yanja's eyes flick over her like the tongue of a rock lizard, testing and tasting. "Greatclan Watch," hshe e says, "I have the Greatclan Lord's own daughter with me. If you bring the *Unfortunate Wanderer* down, she'll die with me."

An airless moment. The frequency crystal flashes. The

Watch warrior says, "The Greatclan Lord has no more daughters."

Yanja curses and fumbles with the pilot's yoke. The cold of the warrior's words are slow to penetrate Atuale's heart. Before she can either freeze or push them aside for the space she needs to thaw, the ship drops out from beneath her.

Below, the ocean pitches wide as they free-fall—in sudden silence. The roar of the engines no longer fills the background of her attention. She would have rather crashed onto land. Returning her body to the ocean is a surrender she would never have chosen. But there is so little land on this world, and so very much sea—

A vicious vibration shudders the tailspinning ship. "Ha!" Yanja crows, and slams his palm on a console. The engines scream as he yanks back on the yoke. Atuale expects the ship to wrench apart under the opposing forces of thrust and gravity—or if not the ship, then her own straining rib cage. But instead the *Wanderer*'s course levels off and it cants skyward once more. Atuale's nails rake her thighs through the thick fabric of her suit as she waits for death or answers, whichever comes first.

"Unknown vessel, return to sea level!" The voice from the frequency crystal cracks. "You lowclan barnacle, get back here!"

Another set of vibrations shakes them, but weaker this

time, farther: enough only to rattle Atuale's teeth.

"What are you going to do at this range, Greatclan Watch? Tickle us to death?" Yanja spins the frequency crystal out of tune without waiting for an answer, and the ship reaches for the heavens.

"Is that why you wanted me to come?" Her voice slithers rough and raw out of her throat. Was she screaming during the descent? She doesn't remember that. If she presses against the restraints with all her might, she can only just see the blue below and, speckled here and there, the scattered archipelagoes of the Vo. Unseen forces shove her back, though, and she wearies quickly. "Because you thought the Watch wouldn't shoot at me?"

Yanja's lips draw back. "Some insurance you are." It's not an answer to her question, but it's as close to one as Yanja is likely to offer. He eases up on the yoke as the vibrant blue of the sky bleeds away into darkness.

The extra pressure sloughs off of Atuale slowly as she takes in the nearness of the stars, the sun. The distance of the world behind her.

She really has left without saying goodbye.

By the time gravity has abandoned them completely, so has the last meal Atuale ate on her way down the cliff.

The sickly acid smell still lingers, though Yanja collects all the floating vomitus with a small hand-vacuum before it spreads too far around the ship. "Egg-eaters," he says as he works, frequently and with a great deal of bile. His dexterity in free-float is impressive, despite the circumstances. She came to the land to learn how to run on her own feet, but in the meantime, he has taught himself to fly.

After he disposes of the waste, he programs something into the console. "Before I set a course for the jumpweb gate, I need to do a visual check on the outside of the *Wanderer*—make sure your father's friends didn't shake loose anything we can't do without. Do you think you can keep yourself from imploding the ship if you're left to your own devices in here?" His teeth gleam when his lip lifts in a sneer. "I'm not risking my neck trying to keep you tethered on untrained extravehicular activity."

"I'm fine." Atuale folds her arms. "Do what you need to do."

"I'll be back soon." He pushes away into a somersault but catches himself on a loop anchored to the ceiling. "You don't need to stay buckled in all the way to Farong, you know. If nothing else I certainly hope you take the opportunity for toileting between here and there."

". . . Thank you." Atuale waits till he flips away again before reaching for the buckles across her chest. The mere action of pressing her shoulders against the seat to slide her arms free sends her sailing upward; she gasps and flings up her hands to ward off the ceiling. Again she rebounds, more gently this time, and a tentative kick sends her arcing out into the ship.

There are long narrow windows set into the upper walls of the *Unfortunate Wanderer,* and as she drifts past them, moving alongside familiar stars, Atuale has the irrepressible impression that *she* is the spaceship in flight. She laughs, and blinks hard, and a new constellation of glittering diamonds swirls up to join her. She catches another of the ceiling handholds and oscillates there, caught up in the moment's wonder.

Out of the corner of her eye, she catches a flicker of movement: the inside lock of the ship, opening wide. Yanja floats in front of it, one hand on the control panel. Watching her. He breaks the stare by ducking his head into a helmet that seals against the wide collar of his suit, and kicks into the lock before it closes between him and Atuale.

She drifts in embarrassment for only a moment. There is something both strange and familiar about the sensation of zero gravity, and the combination is intoxicating. It's like being back under the sea, but without the attendant weight and pressure of a quarter kilometer of water over her head. She no longer has the biological equipment for deep-sea diving, but she is whole enough here.

She wishes Saareval were here, so that she could share the sweet strangeness. A joy divided is a joy doubled, as the Vo like to say. Maybe someday, when he is made whole again, they will walk the way between worlds together. Even if spaceflight did not prove to be the sort of pleasure fitted to the contours of Saareval's heart, surely he would smile to see how it filled Atuale's. A sharp pang jolts the inside of her cheek where she's bit it. A joy divided is one thing, a joy wasted on what cannot be is something else entirely. She makes a few tentative efforts at swimming, which are less than successful—pulling against the empty air gets her even less far than she made it paddling toward Yanja's front door with unwebbed hands and dense unpadded body. But she learns quickly how to push off from the cabin wall with a hand or foot and send herself arcing gently, weightlessly, from side to side.

She's already forgotten Yanja and his business outside the ship when the lock gapes open beside her and blasts her with a breath of subzero air. Before she can roll out of the way, Yanja brushes past. Her knuckles scrape the sleeve of his suit and burn with the terrible cold. "How does it look out there?" she asks, and cradles the hand against herself until it warms.

"Nothing I couldn't fix." His fingers find an invisible

seam and the suit parts over his shoulders. A strange urge passes over Atuale, to lay a hand between his shoulder blades and see if his flesh has chilled to match the impossibly cold suit. "I'll send your family an invoice for the parts I had to use when this all is said and done."

"I'm sure." Atuale looks away from the hard lines of his body. The last time she saw Yanja, the World-Witch was in confinement, disallowed from travel while soft and replete with spawn. Bred by order of the Greatclan, onto—who was it?—a few of the younger princes from the western clans. She blinks rapidly, dissolving the image of Yanja-past. This Yanja is more himself than that silent, gravid ghost. Or perhaps that is only the fog of memory clouding Atuale's vision. "Does that mean we can be on our way?"

"As impatient as ever." His smile curves sharply. "To the gate, then."

Atuale abandons her free-fall dance to strap back into her seat at the front of the ship. Her eyes scrape the stars for the first signs of the gate, though Yanja reminds her more than once that the ship will detect the gate radiation before she ever can. Finally, long after the console has pinged to warn them of their approach, she catches sight of the first of the gate nodes. There are eight in total, Yanja explains, though Atuale can make out only six, the farthest two of which fade to mere specks at their distance. If she looks past them, she sees only more stars. "Different stars," Yanja swears, and she has to take his word for it. All her childhood education seems like a fairy tale now, the otherworlds that modified humans for life on myriad planets nothing more than someone else's often recounted dream.

Yanja counts down their final approach. "Four . . . three . . . two . . ." And just like that, the ship slides through. The stars at the periphery of Atuale's vision shift dizzyingly, but those ahead of her, the ones she's been watching as they approached the gate—those haven't moved, of course. After the bottomless joy of freedom from gravity, the gate jump is shockingly anticlimactic.

She jumps when Yanja laughs at the petulant push of her lip. "Oh, little fry." He's shaking his head as he works up a new trajectory on the console. "If every day you're looking for the next thing that'll change your life—what's left in the moments in between?"

Atuale doesn't have an answer, but then of course Yanja wasn't really asking a question. Behind and beneath her, the engines growl to change their course. To steer her that much closer to her goal.

———

Contractions slash Atuale's belly like a knife. The birth is an easy one: she has already dropped three of her litter, and the fourth is well on its way. Yet there is a wrongness to all of this. She flushes water over her gills, hungry for a breath of proper air. This sun-spangled undersea sandbar is her mother's spawning ground, and tradition and instinct agree that this is where she must deliver herself of her own young.

Or tradition decrees this, at least; instinct refuses to catch up and walk in lockstep. Something is missing, the animal parts of Atuale's brain scream, something has been forgotten. Overhead, a wave rolls, shattering the light on her face into smaller pieces yet.

One last contraction rises like a spring tide. Atuale groans and pushes into it, wrapping her arms more tightly into the seaweed that anchors her. Finally her last offspring wriggles free of her. She catches only a glimpse of jet-black fur before the nearest midwife wraps it up in a waxcloth bundle and tucks it under one arm to swim away. Her webbed feet wash lazy currents over Atuale's face. The child will be delivered, of course, to its father's clan, the artisan Tressh of the southern seas, in the agreement bound by his body and Atuale's and under the authority of both of their fathers.

Atuale tries to feel sorrow for the loss, for the spawn she created but will never really know. Grief slips quickly away from her, though, and only a queasy airless sensation remains. She lets go of her seaweed bindings and kicks upward, making for the shallow surface.

When Atuale's eyes grow sticky, she snatches a scrap of sleep wrapped in a body-sized pouch pinned to the wall. By the time she wakes, her lips are chapped from the air blowing out of a vent just over her head. Wriggling out of the sleep-sack squeezes a few muttered complaints about the vent's placement out of her. Yanja doesn't even look up from the book he's perusing. "Dry skin is a hazard of the lifestyle, my dear. Beats suffocation, anyway."

Atuale loses count quickly of minutes and hours. They pass a bit of time eating, but not very much: their "meal" is a thick fish-food paste that she has to squirt out of a tube directly into her mouth. It tastes good enough but doesn't require much in the way of chewing. It's enough to keep her alive.

The ship cuts across systems and slides through more jumpweb gates. They pass close to a brownish world barely striped with blue water; Atuale wonders how they live. Another system hosts a distant blue-white sun, and as they pass by Yanja points out the half-dozen "stars" that are really planets in orbit. "Why don't we stop at one of these?" she asks half a dozen jumps deep into their journey. She's counting the days—counting Saareval's days. Each passing tide carries away more lost Vo souls. "Since they're closer?"

Yanja sighs and sits up in his seat, bouncing lightly against his restraints. He holds up his fingers and ticks them off, one by one. "Deficient technology. Unwillingness to traffic in available currencies. Worse xenophobia than your precious Keita Vo."

"The Vo aren't xenophobic!" Atuale frowns and picks at the rough edge of a knuckle scale. "I live among them, and I'm not one of them."

Yanja clucks. "Still not one of them after all these years?" A click of his restraints and he slides free of his seat. "Then again, it seems you *are* not-Vo-enough to avoid taking ill." Atuale opens her mouth for a sharp remark, but every blade she tries to grab hold of cuts her first. Before she can surface on the sea of her wounded pride, Yanja kicks against the headrest and glides away. "One last jump before Farong. I'm going to get some sleep before we make port."

She bites her tongue on explanations, reasons. Sharpened-spear retorts. "What do I do?" she asks instead. "With the ship? The controls?"

"Sit on your hands so you don't touch anything. I've programmed in the last point, and it can follow the jump-field radiation to make any minute adjustments to our course. In short, it'll fly itself, if you don't interfere." Elastic squeaks as he straps himself into the sleep-sack. "Think you can manage that?"

"Good night," she says flatly, and then feels foolish, for is it even night back home, or at their destination, or by whatever clock such things ought to be measured here and now? Yanja only chuckles, and then Atuale is alone with the stars.

The last gate jump comes and goes as silently as the first: only a flicker in the periphery of her vision signals her that something has changed. If she cranes her neck she can just make out what she thinks is the nearest gate node, receding into the distance. Disappointment gutters in her belly; she extinguishes it under a breathless push of hope, of necessity, of purpose. She turns the other way, angling for a glimpse of the planet where Yanja hopes to find help.

But there's no planet out there. The air squeezes from her lungs under a tight band of amazement. "What is that?" she breathes, unable to stay silent but unwilling to wake Yanja. She wants this moment alone, to commune with the wonder in front of her.

There's a star somewhere in the middle, she's almost certain of that, an impossible glow that leaks out here and there through the gaps. But wide bands of some material—metal? surely it must be, what other substance could serve?—wrap their arms around and around its light in an impossible knot. On the outside surface of those strips are nodes, nodules, where lights glimmer more warmly than any stars Atuale has seen. Can people really live in such a place? Her heart skips again. *Do* people live here? Or is this an altogether alien place, populated by bodies built to an incomprehensible plan, minds that do not reckon on the same scales and planes as Atuale's?

"You know," says a voice, warm against her ear, "if you hadn't chained yourself to the Vo and their sand-blasted hellscape, you could see sights like this all the time. This is hardly even the strangest place I've been in my travels."

"It's not a chain." The silent communion of the moment has shattered; Atuale blinks and looks away from the unknown world that lies ahead. "It's an anchor." That's not quite right. She loves the bright warm sun of the Vo world, the equity baked into each brick of their social structures. And yet. She corrects herself: "*He* is my anchor."

Yanja laughs, and his hot breath rolls down the curve of her neck before he slides past her into his own seat. "An anchor's a burden for those who have a destination to make."

"But it's a blessing in a storm." And when there is both a storm and a destination to desire—what then? She tries to picture Saareval buckled into the seat beside her, and cannot quite make the image fit. Like her, he has his own private longings, hurts that he thinks he has hidden from her. Ways he believes he has failed her. Only let him live, and they will find a way to shape words to their wounds. They will find a way to heal, or if not that, to soften the scars that linger.

The frequency crystal glows faintly at Yanja's touch. "Farong Nearpoint Intake, this is the vessel *Unfortunate Wanderer,* under the command of Captain Yanja Isk. Do you require registration data?"

Atuale leans into her restraint until it cuts into the scales of her shoulders, waiting for an answer. These people are strangers and simply strange as well: space-dwellers, star-tamers. If they can do such things, what illness could they not heal? What wounds could they not mend?

Sparks pop in the periphery of her vision by the time the crystal glimmers in response. "Captain. Apologies for the delay; I had to update the Marat language module." There is a slight strangeness to the speech, pauses amid words and between them, that signals to Atuale that the words arrive via machine intelligence rather than directly from the intake officer on the other end of the line. The grammar, however, is impeccable enough to pass in the Greatclan halls, and the accent is pure southern clan. "This is Farong Nearpoint Intake. What is your system of origin?"

There Yanja hesitates. He flicks a finger over the console, running down a list of some kind. "We're here from Vancis Voyr."

"Transmit your navigation data."

Yanja sucks on his teeth. He turns, looks at Atuale through lowered lashes. "All right. We're coming from Maraven, as you seem to have surmised."

It takes Atuale a moment to understand that Maraven is someone else's name for the planet on which she has lived her entire life, the place she has only ever thought of as *the world*. The Farong Nearpoint Intake officer, heedless of her revelation, says, "Travel from Maraven is interdicted throughout Ooyet Treaty space. If you still desire to come onstation, you may submit yourself to a quarantine period of no less than two weeks, after which you may submit an entry application under the subheading of 'Refugee Status, Disease or Famine.' If you require additional food supplies during the quarantine period—"

"Two weeks!" Atuale cries. Her arm slashes out, a gesture of denial, but of course the intake officer cannot see. "My husband and his family will be dead in two weeks!"

"We cannot risk the integrity of Farong." The machine-generated syllables roll out of the crystal with preprogrammed inevitability. "We are sorry for your loss. But many human diseases are cross-reactive to other variants. We can't risk the lives of the millions of sentients that live here."

Hope evaporates too quickly for Atuale to grasp it, force it back down into her breast. For a moment she forgets to breathe, like a youngling lifting her head clear of the water for the first time. When the air comes back, it breaks out of her, half gasp, half sob. How stupid, how childish, to trust a path that seemed clear from a distance. "S-samples," she stammers breathlessly, "we have samples on board, we could leave the package in the airlock and you could come and get it and—"

"We don't allow civilians to transport biohazard materials onstation." Is that statement issued with sadness? Irritation? Atuale grasps for a sense of emotion across the great distance between them. It's suddenly, desperately important that she know whether she ought to hate this person or empathize with their struggle to comply with cold regulations. "We've cleared a docking anchor for you: Lower Nearpoint, anchor thirty-two. The anchors are marked in our local language as well as K'lil, Barrakenni, and Ssp. Will you be able to recognize any of those?"

"I've been here before," Yanja says.

The officer seems to accept that as a meaningful answer. "Please attach as soon as possible to keep lanes clear for other traffic. Keep in contact with station personnel; we can provide you with food, as previously stated, and medications if you require them. Do you acknowledge?"

"We acknowledge." Yanja sweeps his hand over the crystal and its inner light fades.

They make their way to the indicated docking anchor in silence. Yanja maneuvers the ship into position—backward, somehow, so that the airlock aligns with the magnetized anchor and its entry port. Its *sealed* entry port.

"It's not fair," Atuale says when Yanja has released his restraints. "We came so far." She digs her knuckles against her eyes and sends another constellation spinning free. When she drags her hand through to clear the diamond-dust of her tears, they shatter coldly against her palm.

Yanja shrugs against his restraints. "*Fair* rarely comes into it, I think you'll find."

"There has to be another way. Another system with strong biotechnology."

"Ea is the next closest and it's still another six gate jumps away." Yanja goes on as Atuale's shoulders slump, "Farong would probably refuel us if we groveled to their satisfaction, but that still puts Ea another week's travel out. Longer yet, on the return trip. And that's presuming first of all that all the gates are in working order, and secondly that the same exact thing wouldn't happen if we go knocking at *their* door. Ea's inside the edge of Ooyet space." His head tips forward and he sighs into the hollow space of his hands. "Word travels fast. Faster still when it comes to things like this."

The airless silence rings in Atuale's ears. Then Yanja ventures again: "There's one more thing. Two gate jumps in a different orientation would take us to one of the secondary worlds of the T't't't."

"The Tkkh—" Atuale struggles over the explosive exhalation that separates each syllable. "The what? Who is that?"

"Another species of sentients. Two, actually, it's a symbiotic relationship. Or so I'm told. I've never met one face-to-face and I can't say if I did I would start off with questions on physiognomy." Yanja turns to her. The stillness of his gaze, without the usual animated dart of his eyes, the twitch of a would-be smile, pins her in place. "They're certainly technologically advanced, though whether they dabble in human health I've no idea. Some gene-eater tech is based on T't't't nanotechnology, although no one knows if they even have DNA themselves. They've been known to be extravagant with gifts to visitors—atmosphere's anoxic, but there are receiving centers for human guests. They're quite accommodating, when they feel like it." He spreads his empty palms wide. "They've also been known, on occasion, to shoot unannounced arrivals out of the sky. They're not human; they can't be expected to communicate like humans. Gods know actual humans can't even manage that most of the time. But I've never chanced it myself. Before now."

Atuale chews on the sweet rich fat of that idea. Interacting with other sentients, seeing with her own eyes an otherworld that few other humans have visited, walking on it with her own feet. In her chest her heart skitters over its beats, trying to regain a steady rhythm.

Yanja reads hesitation into her silence. "Or," he ventures, "we can wait. Two weeks isn't forever. The technopriests of Farong's Undergray—collective? neighborhood? whatever they call themselves—they'll know we're here sooner or later. Who knows? They may already be working on a cure."

"If they knew—if they know—" Atuale strains against her restraints and against the cold, hard edges of an idea at the same time. The pressure of that two weeks crushes down on the rest of her thoughts, leaving them powder-fine and too hard to grasp. Saareval has six days left. Eight, if he is strong. As he has so often been when she needs it. "Why haven't they *done* anything to help?"

"Why not? A host of reasons." Yanja's disdain stings, though Atuale isn't sure if it's directed at her or outward. "Insularity. Stinginess. Ethical codes that forbid interference in the self-development of individual systems. The gods of Undergray are very keen on technological charity and healing and merciful beneficence to the smallworlds. I imagine those moon-eyed martyrs would already be arming a rescue fleet with dermis plasts and nano-scrubbers to send home—if they could. But they're just one small unit of a much greater whole here." He screws up his mouth as if to spit. "The prevailing sensibility across the known worlds is that human variant civilizations are a zero-sum game that one can only win if the others die out and disappear."

"The Vo aren't going to die out!" Atuale finds herself shouting, and lowers her voice. "I don't see how you can say such things as if—as if you're rattling off a storm report or a fishing take."

"Forgive me for not shedding tears over a people who view me as mainly a dispenser for otherworld trinkets." Yanja fiddles with something on the console, and sighs again. He sounds tired, sinking into the same weariness that threatens to drag Atuale down into its lightless depths. "You asked a question. I answered it."

No. Atuale will not be so easily capsized. She opens her mouth to tell him to cut loose from the station and take her to the T't't't.... The risk, though, the risk is so great: if she and Yanja die in the light of an alien sun, torn apart to mere atoms, then who will save the Vo? Who will tell Saareval that she tried, and failed, and loved him to the last? Atuale tastes blood and releases her cheek from between her teeth. The strangeness sings to her. But if she must beg help, perhaps she should ask it of humans, to whom she can try to show the fear-torn ruins of her heart. Who might see that, and understand. "What do you think we should do?" she asks, and her voice is small and high.

But Yanja only shakes his head. "No. Oh, no. This is your little quest, not mine. Have you forgotten all the crèche-stories you grew up on? A Witch may provide the way, but the story's hero must choose it and take it." He shifts like a sea-serpent striking. Atuale flinches, but he only lays a hand upon hers. It is soft and warm, with hard sinews shifting beneath like kraken in the depths. He strokes the backs of her fingers once, twice, and then snatches his hand back as if he is the one who has been burned. It has been such a long time since they have touched one another that way. "Think about it."

When he lets go her skin aches with the cold. Kindness from Yanja? She doesn't know what to do with this, where to put it in her heart.

She closes her eyes and begs the gods of her childhood for answers. Either they can't hear her, so far away, or they have nothing to say to her.

She knows what she would choose. But it is not her life that hangs in the balance. It is Saareval's life, and so Saareval's choice, made by proxy. Safe and familiar as a long-healed scar.

Yanja startles when her hand falls on his shoulder. His hand shoots out, clasping her by the back of the neck, and his face is suddenly too close, his thoughts thrown open wide by idleness. His fingers twist in her mane, but he lets go when she pushes back. She bounces lightly against the far wall and their gazes slide past one another. "Tell me more about this Undergray," she says.

———

Yanja hunches over the frequency crystal, caressing shifts in bandwidth out of it. "No," he says to each wordless crackle and hiss, and flicks his fingers again. "No. No."

Atuale drifts behind the seats. The desire to help stretches painfully in her chest, but she holds it down, locks it inside her, with small, shallow breaths. She knows Yanja well enough to stay out of the way now.

Another sweep of his hand and the crystal emits an inhuman howl. He pauses, and Atuale looks over, hope pulling her shoulders high and tight. But this sound too resolves quickly into mere static. "No," he repeats. His neck pops and cracks when he stretches it. "It's possible there's no one using the sector-assigned bands anymore. The way tech changes here, there's no guarantee anyone's even listening."

The frequency crystal pulses arrhythmically at the

edge of Atuale's sight. "Keep trying," she says. Not a command; she has never spoken to Yanja as the Greatclan Lord's daughter to a lesser vassal. Not a plea, either. An encouragement, then. "For a little while longer. Keep trying."

His lips press flat, but he bends to the crystal again. Another stroke, and the tide of white noise ebbs and flows. Another, and—

Gibberish bursts out of the crystal, an unintelligible chattering. An unintelligible and undeniably human chattering. Yanja shakes his head at the staccato speech and shouts into the first pause for breath: *"Marav! Marav! Balat at mut!"*

The pause draws longer, then dissolves into a crackle. Atuale opens her mouth to insist that Yanja chase down the lost speaker. Before she gets a word out, the voice is back, but altered, modulated and electric. "Well, as I was saying, if you would hold a frequency for more than a millisecond you might have more luck. This is Undergray speaking. Who is this? If this is another prank from you lot in Sixhaven—"

"We're not on Farong at all," Yanja interrupts. "This is the vessel *Unfortunate Wanderer,* and I guarantee you, we are genuine Maraveni."

"Oh? I've never met a Maraveni myself. But it looks here as though your dialectical specificity is very good.

And the transmission artifacts are a nearly perfect match for Maraven's last recorded tech levels." A pause. "You said you were transmitting from a vessel outside Farong? Why aren't you going through one of the intake points? That's protocol."

Yanja hisses and kicks away from the crystal. "*You* talk. You're sad. They'll like that."

Atuale scrambles for the console, clumsy with weightlessness. "I'm just a Technical Initiate," the voice goes on, "really I'm not authorized for primary interciv contact—"

"We need help." Atuale's mane spills over her shoulder; it crackles where it brushes up against the crystal. She catches it and twists it between her hands, to give them something to do. "We're from Maraven, which is dealing with a plague. We already spoke with the intake officers, but they quarantined us for two weeks." The length of time turns her stomach anew. "My people are sick. We'll lose so many, waiting that long."

The voice hesitates. "That seems bad."

Yanja rolls his eyes and twitches two fingers together in an old lowclan gesture: *all the spine of a wet-worm and half the brain.* Atuale pulls herself sideways, floating over the seats, to put her back to him. "My husband is back there," she tells her own reflections, scattered among the crystal's facets. It's easier with a face to say it to. Not easy, but easier. "He's dying."

"...I'm sorry."

The silence that ensues pours into Atuale and fills her with something darker and uglier than grief. She raises her fist as if she would strike the frequency crystal; a click of Yanja's tongue stops her short. "That's it, then? You won't help us?"

"No! I mean, yes—I mean, I will help. I was—I *am*—I'm thinking." The voice hums tunelessly. Atuale twists her hair hard enough to break several strands, which float away when she opens her palm. "Let's see. Let's see. Oh! Well. First of all, are *you* sick?"

The anger that filled her so fast is slow to ebb away. It turns, instead, inward. "No. I'm not really..." Atuale sucks on her teeth. "Neither of us is from the affected human variant. I don't know if we can carry the disease, but we're not ill. We brought samples, though: blood, skin scales."

"I have a transit pod," Yanja says loudly. "If you have a port to receive such a thing."

"Yes, yes, of course. That's good! That's much easier than trying to smuggle you aboard." The voice laughs, then cuts off short, as if their contact has just remembered the reasons for such scheming. "My second orthogonal spouse is biotech dominant and he was just ordained last month, so access to facilities shouldn't be a concern."

Yanja floats up beside Atuale, occupying a large swath of her peripheral vision. "It's considered healthy to have at least one marriage outside your primary discipline," he whispers in her ear. His breath is sour with fruit-paste from the morning meal, a lifetime ago. He speaks louder for the crystal again. "Send us a heading for the transit pod."

"Done," the voice announces confidently, and a light flashes on the console. Atuale reaches out to touch it, but Yanja knocks her hand lightly away. "Biotech and nano aren't my specialty, but Nessik is brilliant. We'll have something for you as soon as we can. Is this frequency all right to contact you on again?"

"Yes, of course." More tears have crept up on Atuale; she swallows them. It is still too early for relief or gratitude. She puts one hand over her heart, as if that will keep it inside her chest. "Before you go, may I ask—what is your name?"

"Magxi," the voice says. "You can call me Magxi."

"Thank you, Technical Initiate Magxi. My name is Atuale."

"Atuale," Magxi repeats. "It's my honor to serve in all the capacities the gods have granted me." The crystal emits one brief shriek, which dies away into faint static that tickles Atuale's ears.

Yanja's transit pod is smaller than Atuale expected: the length of one arm, perhaps a bit less, a tapered rectangle. "Yes, it's for black market trades, and no, I won't tell you what I've had in here."

The generous interior can easily hold all her precious samples, wrapped and rewrapped as they are in layers of protective crabweb netting. Still, Yanja separates out one vial of each kind and nudges the rest back into their shipboard cubby. "You never know, with the Undergray. They love asking questions even more than answering them, sometimes. Best not to give them too many toys to play with so that our little biotech friend doesn't get distracted trying to resolve a complete Vo protein biosynthesis dynamic scheme or some such equally useless thing."

"All right." Atuale looks into the almost empty chamber, with its two lonely vials firmly tucked into a side casing. She half wants to curl herself up small and crawl in alongside them. "I trust you."

A tension snaps Yanja's shoulders high and hard at that remark. "Stand back," he says. "Before you lose a finger." He locks the case shut and seals the edges, then maneuvers it to the airlock.

Though already in zero-g, Atuale finds herself a little

lighter, the inertia of burden reduced ever so slightly. She lays a hand on the case once, bidding farewell, then steps aside to let the doors cycle closed. The outside doors open, the air inside the lock boils. A faint glow of propulsors burns through the white fog, and the case flings itself out into the nothingness beyond. "Swim fast," she says. "Swim true."

"Swim—" The last part of the blessing goes unsaid. Yanja breaks it off with a curse as a bright light flares through the ship's windows.

Atuale flings up an arm to shade her eyes, but the light is already gone. Metallic pings chime against the ship's exterior, like ice shards breaking on rock. "What was that?" she asks. But she already knows, for the gravity of fear and doubt already has her back in its grasp.

The frequency crystal flashes, a pale echo of the blaze outside. Before Yanja can reach it, a voice crashes out of it, sending him and Atuale reeling. "Vessel *Unfortunate Wanderer,* we have detected propulsion fire from your location. This is your only warning. If you attempt to break quarantine a second time, we will sever umbilical support, whereupon you will be permanently refused boarding."

The crystal sputters and goes dark. Atuale's heart flutters like a beached fish's gills: suffocating, fragile. She ought to say the funeral rites, for that was a small piece of

Saareval's life that she has consigned to the void forever. But the Vo words do not come to her; for all the years of speaking and even thinking that language, it escapes her now.

She never did manage to dream in Vo.

The seaclan tongue seeps out of her from some dark, forgotten place. "It was the engines. They saw the engines."

"Yes." Yanja uses the Vo word. He is looking at her sidelong; his fingers rub against his own palms. When he speaks again, he does so in the seaclan language. "Atuale. Are you all right?"

Her eyes are heavy, half-lidded. She is groping her way forward now, feeling the shape of the future and changing it with her hands.

"We have to go to them," she says, and saying it makes it so.

———————

They work in silence at first, sliding into helmets, digging through Yanja's stowage compartments for what they need. Yanja, face furrowed in a terrible scowl, casts unwanted objects over his shoulder without a second glance. Freed from storage, these things float gently through the ship like an asteroid field. Occasionally one bumps Atuale's shoulder, a polite nudge for attention. As often as not she finds herself catching them, turning them this way or that, trying to figure out what they are: this one a tool with some unknown function, that one a musical instrument, this one a pot of blue face-paint with a complicated clasp. For each one, a burgeoning question rises in her gorge, only to be strangled by urgency, necessity. It is pleasant to think that there may be a time for such questions later. Foolish, perhaps, but still pleasant. Atuale's grasp lingers on a pearlpaper scarf, before she lets it slide between her fingers to join its brethren.

Finally Yanja has accumulated everything he thinks they will need, and stowed it in a series of packs and pouches, all laced together. Last of all Atuale puts her precious cache of stealthily collected samples, protectively swaddled in their case, and folds the pack cover over it like a prayer. She holds the whole thing to her chest, and hooks the toes of her suit on the raised edge of a panel to anchor herself in place before she looks Yanja in the eye. Their helmets click lightly, one against the other. "Just me," she says. "I should go alone." The words echo through the helmet plate, through her very bones.

"You? Alone?" Yanja's lips peel back from his teeth and the helmets rattle together harder this time when he pushes against the compartment door to hover over her. "You have to get inside. You have to make them understand what you want. You have to make them put you in contact with the Undergray. How many languages do you speak? How much interciv etiquette are you familiar with?" He laughs darkly. "How much do you know about operating the lightblade you currently hold in your delicate possession?"

Uncertainty tips her head downward, her gaze falling to the pack in her arms. Yanja moves past her without waiting for an answer, a satellite flying too fast to hold in her orbit for long.

That doesn't make him right.

"If I fail . . ." she says. Admitting that raw possibility scrapes the inside of her throat raw. "If I fail, then you're still here to try again. One last time. With another human civilization, or those aliens, the—the T't't't? If we're both arrested, or if we both die here . . ." She stumbles on those last words. *If we both die.* Did she guess, when she set foot on that rocky path down to the sea, that she might be writing her own funeral-elegy? Should she have left a lingering goodbye kiss on Saareval's sleeping brow; should she have stayed a moment longer in the shadows of her adopted Vo city? Death is yet another unexplored horizon, though one she would just as soon hold off on peering past. She squeezes the pack against her chest, as if in an embrace. "It can't end here. Someone has to go on. To save the Vo."

"To save a contract," Yanja corrects, but when her gaze pierces him, his sneer slides away. "I could be the one to go, then."

"And if something happens to you? I can't fly your ship." She would if she could. There is nothing she would not try. Though she would not like to fly it alone.

Yanja tries one last line of argument, and his black eyes shine with things Atuale dares not name. "What if it doesn't matter? What if the Vo are doomed, one way or another? You say it can't end here, but what is an ending?" There's the glimmer again, of something sharp beneath the smooth surface, of the Yanja that Atuale has come to expect if not to understand. "When the deepwhales die, the littlefolk and their herds make homes in the carcasses."

She holds out her hand and he takes it, pulling her upward, setting them both spinning together. "Show me what to do," she says in the apogee of their quiet orbit. "And I will do what needs to be done."

"You will do what you like." His mouth is tight; his eyes have lost their shine. "As you always have."

He shows her the cutting tool whose jaws can make a mince of even the thickest plating; he shows her the spare air-tanks and the tiny little engine pack that she must wear about her waist like a belt. He shows her how to control the internal environment of her suit with certain patterns of tongue clicks, so that she can maintain her temperature when the airless void around her would steal her lifeblood warmth. He tells her a little of the customs of the Faron Agai, the dominant culture in this part of Farong Nearpoint, but quickly throws up his hands in surrender. "How much can I tell you in ten minutes, an hour, a day, that will matter? You grew up in the seaclans and still you flouted our mores as easily as breathing."

She does not rise to the bait and he does not offer another such barbed hook. Finally he is floating beside her as the near airlock doors groan open. Weightless though it is, the pack feels heavy on her back, and its straps pull at her armpits, as if it has different ideas about how she ought to proceed now. Her hands tremble when she tugs them back into a comfortable position. She hopes Yanja does not notice.

"Well," says Yanja, who has shed his helmet. With the extra layer of glass gone between them, his voice is too close in her ear. "If someone has to do something foolish and brave, you are the one with the appropriate experience."

His hand lands in the middle of her back and he pushes. The move propels her forward. She spins gently around one shoulder, but her heart is slamming against the sides of her chest, searching for an escape. And when her rotation turns her around, Yanja is moving in the opposite direction. Backward, away from her and from Farong Nearpoint too.

She catches a handhold over her head and steadies herself. The first time she grabs for the controls, she fumbles and the inner doors only spasm. A breath to steady herself and she manages to key in the command correctly. The doors close on the *Unfortunate Wanderer,* leaving Atuale alone. For a moment, her entire world is a small gray-black box made up of closed doors ahead and behind. She keeps breathing into the moment, hard and fast enough now that the moisture-attracting fabric in her helmet collar can't keep up and the glass in front of her mouth grows opaque with steam.

A small blue light illuminates on the panel when the inner door is fully sealed. No hesitation this time before she keys in the next sequence. The outer doors cycle open, and as the air rushes out it sucks away the sound of its own movement. Atuale follows.

Farong's skin is so close, filling Atuale's view through the open doors. She touches it and the magnetized fields in her gloves pull her hand flat against it. The sudden yank startles her, but when she jerks back the gloves mercifully hold her fast so that she doesn't spin away into the nothingness outside. She cranes her head back, so that she can see a narrow band of stars between the two gray horizons of ship and station. A half-remembered prayer to the gods of the sea sputters out between her chapped lips: the stars are crushingly near! Atuale puts her face to the station and uses her open-palmed grip on the station to pull herself up toward that open sliver of void.

Small motions, now, as she squeezes out into the open. The suit is doing its best to keep her cool, but her heart—the only sound left to her—thunders in her chest at the scope of the universe all around her. If she moves too fast, launches herself out of reach of the station, she will tumble outward forever. A worse fate by far than dissolving into sea foam to crash forever on the shores of the world.

Of Maraven. There is a name for the place she's from, and sliding that label onto it makes the endless starscape shrink a little around her, takes some of the infinite weight off her shoulders. She wanted to embrace the stars; instead they are embracing her. The experience is as exhilarating as she could have hoped, but the thrill is laced with need and dread. She must keep moving.

There will be more wonders to see on the inside. Terrors, too, perhaps.

She reaches forward, reaches again. Her hands and feet cling to the station, and her body too if she huddles in close enough. Not the docks, Yanja told her. There will be other travelers and Intake Assistance, any of whom might report her to Farong Council. "And worse," he said, his face stretched into a knowing grimace, "no public attention. No outcry."

Time recedes from her as she crawls over the face of the station. When panic rises, she chokes it out with measured breaths. However it may seem with the endless surface rising in front of her, the station is not—cannot be—infinite. Progress is measured in steel seams and bolts, in degrees of curvature and the number of windows carefully skirted. When her suit chimes warningly, she anchors herself with as many points of contact as she can manage by lying flat, and wrangles a fresh oxygen tube out of her pack. The empty tubes she sets free into the void; for a brief moment they become one more faint-twinkling star among all the rest before disappearing from view.

She can't help counting progress against these depleted canisters, too. Three left. Then two. Is she moving fast enough? She dares not move faster; already she fears a misplaced handhold will shear her clean of the station to join the constellation of her empty oxygen tanks.

All the while, she keeps the map Yanja drew for her in her mind and adds herself to the topography. An unexpected irregularity in the carefully planned torus. She has swum in darker currents than this, she reminds herself when the air of another canister grows thin. She will find her way.

She is on the last tube when she finds the nexus he described, and sobs out her joyful relief. No, she must save her breath, she is not yet inside to breathe the human-friendly station air. Inhalations balance against shuddering exhalations as she examines the nexus, an ugly and unloved elbow between two nodes of the station. Again she delves into her pack, not for oxygen this time but for a cylinder of similar size. She turns it this way and that, making sure of which end is which, making sure her grasp is as steady as she can make it, before she sets one tip against the station and slides her thumb up along the side to switch it on.

The lightblade does not simply puncture the skin, as she expected, but slides in slowly until a pop underneath nearly sucks it out of her grasp. She yelps, but the wrist-loop she's secured keeps her from losing the blade and her hope along with it. She guides the blade downward, and its slow progress opens a long line that bleeds light.

She turns the blade to the left. Already she can see through the crack that response-tech has arrived to try to deal with the damage. Nanites crisscross in back-lit webs to gum up the top of the first line Atuale cut. They are designed to deal with the sort of harm that a micro-asteroid can do, not a determined sentient with a knife sharp enough to pierce steelica. She forces the blade steadily upward, back toward her point of origin.

Where it crosses the first line it stops, stuck. The nanotech is *not* steelica and the lightblade does not serve to sever those fine webs as it could with two inches of metal plating. The knife's purpose is spent, but Atuale doesn't let go yet. Instead she grasps it as tightly as she can and slaps the other hand flat against the station outside of the shape she has cut. She swings her feet backward, and for a moment she is certain she has broken away, floating to an airless death with only the nanites to bear witness. Dizziness pounds in her head and steals the edges of her vision.

But no: she is still anchored, however tenuously. This is not over yet. She tightens the muscles of her abdomen and brings her feet forward as hard as she can. Not asking entry politely but demanding it.

The cutout gives way, bouncing back into the small chamber on the other side. An environment room, Yanja called it, though to Atuale's eyes it looks denuded of anything like environmental ambience. Her work has depleted the air inside, but there is no water, no green growing things, no sunlight. Pale panels flicker here and there; pipes gleam with the lace of flash-frozen condensation.

When she looks over her shoulder, nanite webs crisscross the entire gaping triangle she has cut. Guilt flashes through her, though these things are far, far subsentient. She can still help them at their purpose. The magnets in her suit palms grasp the broken wall-piece from the inside, and there is still no gravity to resist her as she hefts the rough-cut triangle against the pull of its inertia. She holds it in place for the long minute it takes for the nanites to complete their work, until the hiss of air returns, the gentle tinkle of the pipes, a high-pitched chiming alarm.

Atuale's inner ear has no strong sense of up or down, but the room was clearly built with one in mind, based on the orientation of panels and pipes. She grasps the rungs of a ladder built into the wall. For a moment she hangs there in a perfect unbroken bubble of anticipation. Then she pulls herself what will have to be upward, toward a hatch in the ceiling. Toward the unknown. Her heartbeat no longer sings its lonely, fast-skipping rhythm in a void of air and noise, but she still hears it over the grind of the hatch-wheel as she forces it open and pulls herself through to the other side.

Gravity reasserts itself so suddenly that Atuale nearly falls back through the hatch. Lights pop and flash against the glass of her helmet; she seizes the hatch opening with both hands and overrules her roiling equilibrium. What sound arrives in her ears has been hammered blunt. She pulls herself up on shaking legs, and blinks up into the strange new world around her.

It's an arcade of some kind, a marketplace or bazaar, perhaps, whose tight-crowded booths and throngs of patrons transcend the language of any individual world even though the goods for sale are nothing recognizable. Atuale stretches her fingers toward an asymmetrical bowl in which pearl-pink vapor swirls, contained despite its lack of cover. At the last second, she pulls back before touching it, lest she break the spell or, worse, contaminate it.

The—woman?—behind the table draws back, rapping the backs of her knuckles together and shaking her head. Her hair is not hair at all but something that looks like ribbon, growing blue and green silken and straight out of her head. She says something whose susurrating syllables fail to penetrate Atuale's understanding, and repeats it, louder but no clearer, when Atuale only holds up her hands helplessly. "I'm sorry," Atuale says, and turns away.

There are so many people here, so many more than any Vo market day. They all move back as Atuale staggers through the bazaar, small people pressing close to larger ones, grasping the forked tails of a coat or the bell-shaped curve of a sleeve. Some are tall and thin, stretched out to fit the gentle gravity of low-mass otherworlds. Others are short and broad. There are fur-coated faces and strange hairless ones, diamond-shaped scales very much like Atuale's and curvate, rough-edged iridescent ones not like hers at all. A few make the same gesture with their knuckles as the first woman did. All of them stare.

Atuale wants to stare, too, but she keeps putting one foot in front of the other. Even if she did not have a pressing deadline, she would have had to tear herself away from the sights and sounds of the marketplace before she would have wanted, in order to eat and drink and sleep. Maybe she could walk these wondrous paths again, one day, if she succeeds now. Maybe she could come back. Saareval wouldn't like it.

But then, Saareval wouldn't like her reasons for being here now either.

Four humans recline around an enormous purple gem-rock, the size of a sea-wolf or bigger; its sides run violet-slick and each of those around it have slender silver straws that run from their lips to the strange liquid. They pull back stray limbs at Atuale's approach, flinch away from her passage. A fifth figure approaches, from Atuale's periphery, faster than she would like; she jumps and spins, only to find something less than human bearing down on her. No, not *less* than human, simply *other than*; concentric rows of pulsating cilia frame a rugose opening from which formless noise issues. Longer cilia snap out at Atuale, sending her stumbling backward, but the tears that rise in her eyes are not of pain or fear but of wonder. A wild urge to pull off her helmet beats fiercely at her breast, to add smell and texture to the sights and sounds that immerse her. She pushes desire away, and looks around, as if she has not already stumbled far off the path that Yanja set her.

A small man steps into her path, pulling her up short. He wears gloves that conceal impossibly long, slender digits, and in his spider-hands he holds up a chain of flowers. The petals are so black they seem to drink down noise as well as sound, or at least the rustle and roar of the bazaar falls away as the man leans in to say in a thick lisping accent, "I know where you come from, far-traveler. My world is a dead one and I wish you well on your way." He leans forward on his toes and throws the flower-loop necklace upward, toward the crest of her helmet.

As black flowers fill her sight, the rustle returns and crescendos into a roar. A mechanical shriek, and Atuale's arms are bound to her sides by rubbery strands that resist her struggle—her old friends the nanites, repackaged for use against her. Voices, artificially loud, echo in the confines of her helmet. Gloved, splayed fingers steal the view through her faceplate as she crashes to the ground. The last thing she glimpses before she is bodily hefted and pulled away is the flower-chain, crushed into a weeping black ocean beneath heavy feet.

———————

Atuale shivers naked in the dark. The green, faintly acid-scented ooze that coats her scales glimmers wetly in the dull light overhead; the cool air blowing out of a vent nips unkindly at the liquid. The room huddles close around her—less of a room than a cell, really, enough space for only a cot and toilet and sink and Atuale and all of her fears.

Her pack is gone. She tried to explain about the samples inside, the precious blood sleeping inside its nest of durafreeze, but her words struck no spark of understanding that she could see. No more than the blared commands of her captors had pierced her own confusion. She has no faces to which she can assign fear, hate, despair; putative emotions roll over her memory of those smooth, blank white masks, and wither without taking root.

There are a few gape-mouthed sores, on her arms and belly, where healthy scales ripped away in the cruel thoroughness of their decontamination procedures. When her mind sets to screaming about all that has receded beyond her reach to impossibility, she picks at these oozing wounds. Perhaps her remaining scales and Saareval's will line up together. A complete set between the two of them. She tries to remember how many he had lost by the time she left, where exactly those lesions had marked him, and whether they matched up to her own.

The sharp scrape of metal on metal cuts through to her. The hatch embedded in her door dilates, and a small oblong object tumbles through. Atuale winces, waiting. But nothing else happens as the hatch contracts. Her breaths chain together, expanding in either direction to fill the empty, endless solitude, waves of time pulsating back to the past, forward into the future. Maybe it's a lifeline. Maybe it's poison.

If it changes the status quo, is there any meaningful difference?

She accepts the thesis set out by the object's arrival: to know is better than to not. Her legs cramp and twinge as she unfolds them—how long has she been curled up atop the cot?—and crawls to the door.

At her touch, the unknown object glimmers yellow. She turns it, and identifies a regular geometric shape inside a cool, clear case.

A frequency crystal?

She strokes the side of the case, trying to find a way to tune it. They can't have given her a lifeline to the world outside with its other end severed. Can they? She strokes again, squeezes it, tries twisting it between her hands.

When finally she lifts it to slam against the wall, as if its case is a block of ice from which she must free it, a voice slips free: "Atuale? Are you there? They said you'd be there."

It takes her a moment to recognize the speaker, distorted by the crystal as he is. "Yanja?" Relief floods over her so suddenly, she is swept away by its current. Her limbs melt. She falls against the floor without catching herself, and tastes blood. There is still hope, however small and faint. There is still a chance, as long as Yanja is there. "They have me locked away, Yanja. All my hopes are hanging on you, now." She tries to keep the note of pleading out of her voice, and fails. "Where are you going to go? What will you do now?"

Silence crackles down through the crystal, lifting the fine hairs between her arm-scales. "The T't't't," he says finally. "Never charted a course through honest-to-gods nonhuman territory before. It would be a thing to see, wouldn't it?"

Would-be is a word for Atuale, whose sea and skies are dull-scraped steel now, whose air is recycled and ripe with her own souring fur-oils. *Will-be* is for Yanja. But she doesn't correct him. "How soon do you need to leave?"

"Refueling's already underway, I'm happy to say. After that, they'll have to check the local traffic and clear me for disconnect. And of course there are a few legal matters to get out of the way first, related to one of my passengers, who may have violated a few local ordinances."

Atuale's fist clenches around the crystal. The rest of her body still splays bonelessly on the floor, all her energy and emotion channeled through five taut fingers. "That was all my fault! They have to blame me!"

"Exactly what I told them. There are still forms to fill out, though, things to sign. A small matter of fine—not to worry, I'll handle that, fault or no."

"The Vo will be thankful for all you've done." Atuale's arm-scales press into her cheek, raising tears in her eyes. "I'm thankful too."

Yanja laughs. "The Vo will resent me all my days for giving them what they couldn't get on their own. But they'll pay me fair, and coin spends better than thanks anyway."

"Still. Please. When you get back, tell Saareval—"

A dismissive click of Yanja's tongue. "I'm already running your errands. I'm not carrying your love notes, too."

"Tell him I'm sorry."

Silence stretches out. Yanja's breathing carries over the frequency crystal, its peaks and valleys amplifying Atuale's own. When his next inhalation hitches, as if he's about to speak, Atuale blurts out the question whose claws are in her heart. "Why did you agree to do it? Come out here, burn your last bridges with the clans? You hate my family and you hate me. You can't love coin all that much."

Even warped by the crystal, the blade of Yanja's voice cuts deep. "And you can't be so curious as to stick your hand into an open flame, yet here we are. Don't ask questions you won't like the answers to."

But there are no answers, to be liked or hated or slowly dissected in the growing silence. Only questions, torn open wide, and an airless void on the other side. Atuale shudders with the first sob, and by the time she has calmed, her own breathing is the only sound left to her.

———————

The stains on the sheets are brown and red, pulsating clouds of blood and amniotic fluids. Atuale twists her fists into the soft fabric. Giving birth under the cruel press of gravity is so different, such an act of endurance compared to the infants she littered under the seas.

Or perhaps it is not gravity's pull that threatens to submerge her now but that of emotion. She wanted this child, wanted it with Saareval, wanted that sense of justice and rightness in her birthing-bed that has been denied to her all along.

Where is Saareval? Dealing with the remains of the infant, perhaps. Mourning. The Vo do not pray, but they have their rituals, their purifications, for dealing with the dead. The never-living. The fetus endured less than half of the way through its gestation, surrendering its grasp on existence before a doctor could take a reliable scan. Would it have been any easier to have this news delivered coolly and clinically by a medical professional than by the vehement rejection of her own body?

A sob grinds into powder under the contractions of Atuale's throat. The midwife, still crouched between her legs, breaks her stoic grimace to look up sympathetically. Her hand rests briefly on Atuale's bare, blood-streaked knee before she returns to her business. Atuale knew, they all knew, that this could happen. That the mods that had remade her somatic cells might not have acted fully upon her ova. That the chromosomes might fail to match up neatly, that the worlds of seaclan and Vo might never be so fully intertwined as to reproduce together.

She looks at the winged nebula of red-black fluids that spreads out on either side of her, and wonders: Is this what was meant to be? And how can that be so?

Sleep steals Atuale away from her condition for only a little while. A banging from outside her cell jolts her awake, and she scrambles to a sit as the door swings outward. Two faceless humans enter—some of the same ones who intercepted her in the marketplace, or others identically dressed. It hardly matters. They bark bewildering orders and gesture sharply until she pieces together the charades-game and stands in the middle of her floor with her hands upon the back of her head. One figure levels what must be a weapon at her as the other approaches. The object is slender and slightly curved, flaring wide at the end nearest her; it looks like no weapon Atuale has ever seen, but the posture of threat is a universal language.

The nearer figure commands her again, a needle-sharp syllable into which Atuale can thread no meaning, and then they are up in her face, reaching around behind her head. She wills herself not to tremble at this invasive nearness. Something touches the back of her neck—lightly at first, then a deep-reaching sting. She cries out, and the figure jumps back to the safety of their companion.

"Don't move!" cries the other, the one with the weapon, and this time there are familiar words overlaying the strange, incomprehensible sounds. She touches the back of her skull with her upraised hands, and finds a small metal rectangle whose teeth bite into her flesh. What wondrous thing is this, that can whisper to her in an alien tongue?

"I won't," she says first, "I won't move." As she hears it now, even her own voice is layered, an echo of her own words translated back upon themselves unaltered. She swallows, and shakes her head to clear it; hearing an echo of herself in her own head fogs up some primal understanding of speech. "What is happening?"

"You'll be brought before the Farong Council for a hearing." The unarmed figure holds up a small canister, spiraled at either end like the spire of a seashell. "This biofilm will reduce the risk of contamination. Do *not* attempt to tear it."

"I wouldn't." She holds out her arms to either side as they direct, and closes her eyes. The canister pops, and a cooling sensation cascades down over her face, her torso, her limbs, even sliding over the soles of her feet when she lifts them one after the other. When she is permitted to look, she wears a second skin of bluish gel, one that follows the contours of her shape and moves when she does. "Thank you," she says, looking between her two captor-guardians.

The armed one gestures to the open door. "Come along."

There are more steps of decontamination, chemical showers and layers of pale powders that absorb into the blue biofilm. The other two figures abandon her for the duration of these ministrations, and only a series of opening doors ushers her onward from one scouring to the next. When at last she emerges into the last chamber, what must be the same two await her, though they have discarded their bulky protective suits in favor of a simple sash and kilt. No need to ward themselves against Atuale any longer, not now that she is severed from their world and bound up inside a tiny blue-tinged universe no bigger than herself.

They are different kinds of humans, the taller one lightly covered in soft white down, the smaller's brown skin bare of fur or feather. It also does not escape Atuale's notice that, now, *both* of them are armed.

Through the bowels of Farong they lead her, along oft turning corridors decorated only with bare, irregularly corrugated metal. So different from the busy halls above—or below, or simply elsewhere? No way to know which way her travels through the station have oriented her. Here, some unnameable fluid drip-drops down from a seam overhead; there, faint light squeezes through a crack in the wall. Is this flimsy machinery all that stands between Atuale and the cold, uncaring vacuum outside? She puts her eye up to the opening, and peers closer at the orange light. It originates in a web of pulsating sacs on the other side—and when Atuale's fingers touch the wall, she finds that it is not metal at all, but some leathery organic material. She yanks her hand back as the guard behind snaps at her to move along.

At last they emerge through a dilated hatch—much like the one in Atuale's cell, albeit far greater in scale—into a vast chamber. The shape of the space is faintly pyramidal, and the walls are irregular with three or four dozen podiums of various heights: some scarcely taller than Atuale's head, and one reaching nearly all the way to the peak of the room, where vines bearing gold-white lamps cast their blazing light on those below. If she cranes her head back, she can see where small figures peer over the edges of those podiums. Some are plainly human, in a rainbow of browns and grays and pinks and yellows; the species origin of others, at this distance, is harder to discern.

"Go on, then." The nearer guard nods at her when she looks over her shoulder at them. "These are the councilors from Nearpoint, Kitefall, Advance Heights, Undergray, and the Scales. They rarely convene all together, but they have for you. They will hear you out and offer what justice may be had."

"For the needs of your people," says the other guard, "and your crimes alike." They give her one last prod with the flared end of their weapon, and she stumbles away as they retreat back to the margins of the room.

Only then does she realize that she is not alone on this vast and brightly lit floor. Another solitary figure, limned in naked blue, waits near the center. His shoulders are turned away from her, his head bowed, but she knows the shape of him.

She raises a fist as she comes up on him, but when he does not turn to confront her, she loses her momentum and her arms fall to her sides. "You said you were going," she hisses. Her vision blurs with tears that have nowhere to go; they squeeze down over her cheekbones and cling beneath the biofilm there. A tiny tidal pool of snot collects on her upper lip. "You said you'd be *gone*."

"I lied. Gods of the deep, you'd think you'd expect that by now." His shoulders jerk up and down, less a shrug than a shudder. His face-paint is gone, scrubbed clean by decontamination. Without it he looks younger, less disdainful than honestly bewildered. "They boarded the *Wanderer* in a spray of decontamination gel just after you sliced your way into their station. Afraid I would get the same fool idea in my head, apparently."

"Who's going to save them now?" she asks, and only then does he look at her over his shoulder. He reaches for her and instinctively she reaches back, and their bodies slide coldly one against the other with the gel layer between them. Under her cheek, his chest is harder than she remembers, but he is still of the right height for her head to nock neatly under his chin.

An amplified voice sends them staggering apart. "The

Council of Justice is now in session," it booms. Atuale looks around wildly for the podium of origin. Only when she cranks her head back to peer at the highest one does she find the speaker. At such a great height, the apical vine-lamps are almost directly behind him, which casts his backlit face in shadow. "You will present your plea. The Council will debate your case. And justice will be handed down to the best of our ability. Do you understand?"

"The samples!" Atuale breaks away from Yanja, standing under the tall podium and its darkness-veiled speaker. "Please! Where are the samples I had?"

Another speaker, from a lower platform, raises her voice. "The diseased blood is under analysis in the temple laboratories of Undergray." She leans forward with her elbows on the edge of her podium and steeples her fingers. Her eyes are not on Atuale but on the chief speaker above. "As they should have been directed immediately upon these pilgrims' arrival."

Though his placement hides the chief speaker's face, his sneer is audible. "The religious beliefs of Undergray cannot be permitted to dictate the protocols that keep the people of this habitat conglomeration safe."

"Perhaps on another day we will bring to a vote a discussion of what constitutes safety and how best to provide it." Undergray's speaker tucks her chin to her chest to look down at Atuale. The scales covering her skin are jet black, though around the eyes and mouth some have lost their color. Her longish face brings an eel to mind, and her darting eyes its sinuous path through the water. "I have been to Maraven, some years ago when I thought I might understand the universe better through seeing as much of it as I could. I remember a kindly welcome from the dwellers beneath the waves, and visiting their pearl-palaces and porcelain great-halls."

Atuale forces words past the thickness in her throat. "The seaclans can be generous." If they thought you might be generous, in turn, with your knowledge or goods or body. "And the Greatclan Lord is always pleased for the opportunity to show his wealth and power."

"Is there a purpose to this anthropology lesson?" asks the chief speaker. Two other low-speakers slap open palms on their desks and rebuke him with hushing sibilance.

Undergray tilts her head, less fish now than curious mammal. One finger pecks at her lower lip. "There was no love lost, as I recall, between the people of the deep-water and those of the dryland, who ignored my en-treaties toward sharing my technology. It surprises me, then, to see the two of you together in this hope of saving the drylanders."

"I was born in the sea and remade for the land." Atuale's hand darts out, finds Yanja's elbow, and slides down to his palm. "My friend found a way for me to move between the worlds. For love." Yanja's fingers seize around hers, and the words skitter across her tongue too fast. "And f-for freedom, too, and for curiosity." The yellow of Undergray's eyes flushes amber at hearing that. Atuale's heart flutters. "I'm the daughter of the one who offered you welcome and plenty." Even though he did not want her to be here—but the Farong Council hardly needed to know that. "For the sake of what goodwill you still bear toward your time on Maraven, for the gods you honor with your knowledge and generosity—"

"And for love." A taut smile pulls the lines of graying scales around Undergray's mouth into arcane angles. "Tell us about the plague, its progression, its symptoms. We will hear you through. Then the Council will talk. Public opinion is mixed, certainly, after your . . . shall we say appearance in the Gathering Halls." The smile broadens. "Magxi sends zir greetings."

"Later," says the chief speaker, "we will discuss the matter of consequences."

His tone chills Atuale, but Undergray ignores him. "I'm certain I am not alone in refusing to turn my back on a world in need. We'll help you, traveler, in what ways we can. Tell us what you know."

Atuale presses her free hand to her heart. "Thank you,"

she says, and searches for the words to start.

———————

When the Council withdraws to deliberate, guards escort Yanja and Atuale back to the shuttle, where they wait together in sharp-bladed silence. Here and there, blobs of decontamination fluid have congealed into pinkish orbs. When they rip away their layers of biofilm, these clot together too and drift ominously through the air. Neither Atuale nor Yanja has the energy to attack this debris with the liquid vacuum. Nor have they bothered to put away the objects dislodged from storage compartments.

Yanja's long hair is wet and sticky with the fragments of the biofilm. "Let me braid it," Atuale says, and when Yanja does not object, she anchors herself around his torso with her legs and combs her fingers through. It's good to be close. It's good to feel something. She wishes he would feel something back at her—that he would say something, sigh, shove her away. She tucks her knees up under his armpits and pulls herself tighter.

She's just finished tying up the plait when the frequency crystal pulses with light and life. "*Unfortunate Wanderer,* are you there?" It is the speaker from Undergray.

Atuale somersaults across the shuttle to activate the

crystal on her end. "We're here. We're listening."

"Excellent." Atuale closes her eyes to imagine Undergray's face-stretching smile. "Several of the finest bio-priests in our order are at work on your problem. They're developing a sort of bionanite—something with which your people can be injected. It will produce a variety of antiviral peptides to combat the virus in its current form as seen in your samples, and it will also be able to react to combat new mutations as needed. We will be able to provide you with a working prototype in . . . I am told six hours, perhaps four if testing runs smoothly."

Bits and pieces of those words wash through the net of Atuale's understanding, but the gist remains: a cure for the Vo. A lifeline for Saareval. If he still lives. She wrings the words out of her clamped throat: "Thank you. Thank you."

Yanja has drifted up behind her. He leans toward the crystal. "We can pay, of course. We have trade goods, and some Farong credit—"

"Your thanks are appreciated, but not necessary, and you will not insult us with further offer of payment." Undergray's chuckle takes the sting out of her words. "It is no less than our duty before the gods, to protect life where it remains. To strengthen our knowledge of the universe they left for us, and to build bridges between our far-flung humanity."

"You are very kind," Atuale says.

The crystal hisses with a sharp intake of breath. "We are very reverent. And before you ascribe any kindness to the people of Farong, there is something else you ought to know."

Later, Atuale will remember this moment, how time and space crowded in too close around her. It's strangely like her passage through the airlock, with closed doors in front and behind and all the air squeezing away. "I've been asked to read this message by the chief speaker on his behalf. Well. You will forgive me, I hope, if I don't go through it verbatim." A cough. "The speaker and the Council Majority are of the opinion that your earlier actions endangered the lives and safety of several million sentients. Their concern is that, based on the precedent you set here . . . they're offering you a choice, you see. To ensure that you don't go on to jeopardize another stationhold, or planet, or such."

"What choice is this?" That's Yanja, not Atuale. She has forgotten how to speak.

"The choice is not your concern, pilot. This was her doing, not yours, and the Council has been convinced to spare you for your proximity to danger." Undergray picks her way carefully over slippery, capricious words. "It is a matter of confinement. That part has not been left to your choice. You may return to Maraven only under the agreement never to leave its atmosphere again. And please understand: Farong Council will not depend on your honor as a sentient to remain landbound. Their ties to other civilizations are strong and plentiful. Breaking your confinement will mean at best an arrest in a similar manner to which you've already been accustomed." She clears her throat. "At worst, any ship upon which you travel will be destroyed before reaching its destination."

Well. That is no great punishment. It is for Saareval that Atuale came; it is to him that she will return. She opens her mouth to accept her sentence.

But Undergray is still speaking. "Otherwise, drylander, you may accept probational citizenship in Farong—where the Council can keep a close eye on your doings." Atuale's heart twists sideways. The view above the window, of the close and glittering lights, expands to fill her heart and mind. She sees herself walking on the arcade, tasting the arcane offerings there, losing herself in the sweet strangeness of alien song.

A choice, Undergray said, but what a strange thing to say. There is what Atuale wants, and there is what Atuale needs, and between the two there is no choice at all. "Back to Maraven. I'll stay there. I promise."

Yanja pushes away from the crystal, toward the back of the ship. Heedless of the din he makes as he starts cramming discarded objects back into their storage—perhaps the crystal cannot pick it up at such a distance—Undergray says, "Yes, I thought that might be the case. Why risk so much, if the world meant so little?" Her voice teems with the warmth and life of the Nearpoint market when she says, "You would have made a good citizen, I think, and a welcome adherent to the temples of Undergray, or whatever sector offered you a calling."

"Thank you," Atuale says again. The phrase rings hollow, scraped empty of meaning by her repetition.

"Farong will be in contact soon to transfer our offering, but I do not expect I will speak to you again. I hope that the life you return to will be a happy one, and that your gods, if you have them, and mine alike will smile on your time there."

She says it one last time: "Thank you." But there is no further sound from the crystal, so perhaps the words never made their way to Undergray, perhaps they will stay trapped in orbit around Farong forever. An appropriate souvenir to leave behind, perhaps. Her heart tears down the middle, between memories of the Maraven-that-was and dreams of the Farong-that-will-never-be. She pushes backward and swims toward Yanja.

Her hand traces the curved line of his spine where he hunches over an open locker. He does not flinch away or lean into the touch, only keeps trying to get the contents of an open bag of biobatteries to stay behind the door

while he shuts it. "This body. Did you let this happen because you thought I would prefer it? With gene-eaters,
you could have—"

"This body is mine. My skin finally fits me right. You
were long gone by then, living like a Vo, marrying into
their families." His lips draw back from the yellowed
crests of his teeth. "I hadn't seen hide nor hair—nor *scale*
of you in twenty years."

"Yanja—"

"*You* left first."

Atuale's breath catches. She spends so much time
curled around the pearl of her own pain that she's forgotten Yanja knows how to hurt, too. "I'm sorry." She
waits a moment, to let that statement settle beneath the
surface of the tension between them. Her palm flattens
against the plane of his back; his vertebrae press back,
like knuckles. "We both put our backs to the sea, but
I went to the Vo and you went to the traders' guilds. I
didn't think you wanted to see me, after I climbed the
stair alone. I thought then that you might follow me. That
was—that was naïve. We have both been looking always
outward, upward. But in different directions. And later,
when the fighting broke above the waves, when I real-
ized the whole time, you'd just wanted to use me against
my father . . . to implode the Greatclan holdings. Gods
know he deserved that. But I didn't." She squeezes her

eyes shut, as if in the darkness behind them she could peer into the past. "Did I?"

She's not asking the right questions, not quite. Yanja can't have *just wanted*, because *just* is an empty, useless word. There's never a *just this*, or an *only that*, when someone does something. It's a web, all tangled together, and the person least likely to unwind it all is the one in the middle. But the concepts she seeks recede from her, and she is left holding only the tattered shreds of a vast idea. Her hand slides up to his shoulder and she pulls. Weightless as he is, she still has to fight his inertia to force him around to face her. "This trip, though. That was for me, wasn't it? You thought I'd taste this life and then thirst for it forever after. Enough to join you in it, maybe."

The lines of his face are inscrutable. "It doesn't matter. Whatever taste you had was poison anyway."

When he goes to turn away, again to the damnable batteries, she yanks him back. "Because it was so short? It was never poison. It was perfect. The things I saw—the people—I saw aliens, did I tell you that, actual aliens?" Dark marks spangle Yanja's face and chest; it takes her a moment to realize that these are the meteor scars of her own tears. "Not poison. Something precious." She takes his hand and settles it over her breastbone. "Something I'll keep close to my heart always, for when I need it."

His fingertips twitch and press in harder, as if he might

dig deeper, tear through her suit, take that heart out, and examine it for the truth of her words. She hisses, but not in pain. Her hands slide up behind his neck and she pulls them together. His lips part around unspoken words before she presses her mouth against his.

All questions asked and answered, with a single kiss, save one. "Saareval," says Yanja against Atuale's open mouth.

"Saareval," Atuale agrees, and closes her eyes on that beloved name. It should feel like a betrayal. Instead, as Yanja's mouth seals promises into the skin of her neck, Atuale has the sense of writing an ending to a book long left unfinished—or if not an ending, then, perhaps, the bridge between two verses of a well-loved song.

Hands tremble with the pressure of twenty years' wait as suits are peeled away. Atuale's scaled limbs whisper letters of long-lost emotion against Yanja's oil-slick fur when she wraps her legs around him. His hands, bigger now than she remembers, find purchase on the muscle under her arms, and he tugs her against him, up and down. His claspers explore the topography of her body before one slides needfully inside. There's a jolt of pain as it anchors itself inside her, quickly washed away by the cocktail of anesthetic and nerve-warming pheromones released by the binding. The same mechanism that anchored generations of their ancestors together beneath the waves now lets them drift not in water but on a heady tide of weightlessness: two orbiting moons accreting into a single, softly spinning body, and the windows are spangled with stars to bear witness.

Atuale does not look back on Farong as it grows small behind them, does not grab for a last souvenir of those glittering strings of light. Until the first gate swallows the ship up, she and Yanja sit side by side in silence: not companionably, exactly, but not the confused coldness of before either. If this moment is a new part of the song, it is one that will need to be rehearsed if it is to become as easy as second nature. She takes out the pot of blue paint and, without asking, reaches across to sweep broad strokes of the electric color beneath his eyebrows, along the curve of his lower lip. He closes his eyes into her touch.

"It's a long way across," says Yanja once she has finished, once he looks like Yanja, her Yanja, again. He adjusts the console minutely, gliding from panel to panel with the confidence of a practiced pipe-player or engineer-artist. "You ought to get some rest, before you go playing nursemaid to an entire subspecies."

"We both should rest." She studies the unfamiliar constellations that shape this particular frame of the universe. "Playing hero to an entire planet is wearisome work."

"Hero!" Yanja snorts. "I still want that contract, you understand. This ship doesn't run on—on—" The thread of the joke unravels there, leaving him frowning into the empty space ahead. Atuale leaves the unsaid words unexamined. Her lips pull into a faint smile, an upside-down mirror to his expression.

Neither of them rises from their seats. The dull hum of the engines below echoes the vibration of their constituent atoms. All things are different and the same and thus interconnected, all things are ever in motion, and the way home can be a great distance and close to hand at the same time. The vacuum of words that stretches between them is filled by her ever-expanding sense of rightness. Of what will have to pass for peace.

Yanja breaks the quiet first. "I'm sure he's fine. Saareval."

"Yes." The universe may be unfamiliar, but it has not turned upside down; this must be so. "I know he is."

"You've loved him a long time." It's something between a question and an accusation. Yanja has spent twenty years thinking she went to the land not with her arms open for an embrace, just with her back turned on the promise of power in the world to which she was raised.

There's that word again, *just,* as fragile and unworthy of the weight placed upon it as ever. "I've loved him a long time, and I've loved him the most." Atuale licks her lips, testingly. A trace of salt lingers on her tongue. "But I loved you first."

In the space between them, their hands float out and fingers twist loosely together. Everything is new and everything is familiar, all at once, a strange kind of balance and an exhausting one. Atuale closes her eyes and gentle sleep comes seeking her company.

They approach the planet from the horizon opposite the Greatclan Lord's holdings. The lesser clans on the opposite hemisphere acknowledge their entry but do not oppose it, and Yanja clings low to the dancing waves as he flies homeward.

He lands on the pad in the Keita Vo marketplace, not at the bottom of the cliffs. Atuale hasn't asked that of him, but relief sings in her anyway. The sensation of weight settles back into her bones all the heavier for her time without it. When she puts it on, the straps of the pack bearing Farong's cure dig heavy into her shoulders; its ballast is lopsided and sends her staggering sideways.

Yanja catches her and redistributes the weight of the pack. His hand lingers on Atuale's belly a moment.

She stills into the moment, thinking he means to slide his fingers lower, ask her to stay without so many words. "You could come with me, you know. Mods or not—you could come for a while, a short one or a long one."

But he lets go with a soft grunt of deferral, and there is no time to tarry over a gentle argument now that the implacable clock of interworld travel has run down. Later, she will wonder if he could smell it on her, if his fingers sought some soft change in her, some confirmation of that instinctive knowledge. For now, she turns her back on him, raises a hand against the dry afternoon sun, and steps down onto the soil of her homeworld.

A few Vo have come out from the shelter of homes and market tarps to watch the ship make landfall. The reek of illness rolls off of them, of the entire town; Atuale's stomach curdles, though she strives for a neutral expression. The stone-faced Vo watch her as she walks down the main street through town, but with their peeling scales come cracks in the mask: some hopeful, some resentful, some painfully unsure.

Atuale opens the door to the shared room of the sister-house. Two of Saareval's siblings and one of his cousins are there, weeping, huddled together on a single divan. On the table in front of them oddments are scattered:

empty pill-vials and open widemouthed jars still rancid with the remnants of holy oils. All three fall silent when Atuale enters. "Where have you been?" asks the cousin, jumping to his feet. He points to the pack on her back. "What is that?"

The younger sister shakes her head. A scale is peeling off her chin; it hangs by a strand and rattles against her jaw when she moves. "He won't thank you for that."

"I'm not here for his gratitude." Atuale has not stopped moving and she does not pause at the open archway into the pairdwellings. "There's more, if you want it, and you'll be only as beholden as you wish." Her foot finds the first stair and she pushes upward, against relentless gravity, against a sudden sense of dread. "If not, keep your thoughts to yourself."

"She can't," the cousin says, "she isn't—" He looks between the other two, as if expecting them to finish his sentence. But neither of them does.

She navigates the warren of pairdwellings with the confidence of long habit. The curtain to her and Saareval's rooms is askew and she slips through it without touching it.

Inside, the smell of sickness and rot is enough to bring bile to her mouth. She gags, and tears burn her eyes.

But ragged breath cuts through the dark and wretchedness, and Atuale stumbles toward the bedside.

She finds Saareval's familiar shape, strokes his face, hushes him when he strives for speech against the fluid in his lungs. "It will be all right," she whispers against the indentation of his ear. Her fingers find the soft, scaleless seam inside his elbow, and she presses a micro-canister of Farong's cure into his skin. "Everything will be all right."

His eyes betray neither forgiveness nor anger; there will be time to navigate a course between those two shores later. But Saareval's withered arms slide around her, and it is good. "I'm not sorry," she tells him.

His words drift to her from the depths of the lymphatic sea that drowns him: "You came back," is all he says.

Sweetwater tears prickle her eyes. She takes his mosaic-patchwork hand and places it on her belly. "My love," she says, and there are so many new notes to the symphony of that word now. "Rest a while. Let me tell you a story."

One day, later, not so very long from now, Saareval will hold her again this way in a tide pool of salt-kissed stones, as three healthy pups press their way free of her body. They will be the children of his heart, if not his body, and their hearts too will be sun-warmed with love for all their parents, though they are the children of the sea, and of the stars too, when they are older and prepared to join their father-Witch in his far-ranging travels.

And whether one day, in that hazy future, one of them might ask their father-Witch for a way to go live for good with their mother and father of the sun and sand—she cannot, dare not, say for certain. But if one should, surely their father-Witch would find a way for it to happen, for there will be no coin more dear to him in the currency of any world than the laughter of his sun-daughters, sea-daughters.

Acknowledgments

Ever since I was a teenager, I've wanted to hold my very own book in my hands. It's surreal and thrilling that it's finally happening! What I didn't know then, though, is that it takes a village to raise a book, and I'm very thankful to have such a smart, kind, thoughtful village behind this one. I'm grateful for the Codex members who read it in its infancy, as well as the incisive critique from my second readers—Lina Rather, Jordan Kurella, Meábh de Brún, and of course Bennett North, my frequent partner in literary crime, who talked me off many a ledge with this book. I'm grateful to my Viable Paradise instructors and classmates; my experience with them helped me figure out how to get the story where it needed to be. I'm grateful for the team at Tordotcom Publishing, starting with my brilliant editor Christie Yant, who took a chance on this story with me and who had a vision for how to take the story to the next level; to Lee Harris, Ruoxi Chen, and font of publishing information and know-how Emily Goldman; Chase Stone, the cover artist who made the book pretty on the outside; and Sona Vogel, the copyeditor who made it match on the inside, and all the other people working hard in the background of books like this one.

I'm so very grateful for my wonderful spouse, Andrew, who supported me along the way; my in-laws, Dale, John, and Cecily, who spent time with my children and thus bought me hours to write and revise; and my two beautiful babies who were so often patient when Mommy needed to sit down and clatter away on the YouTube machine for a while. Thanks, kiddos, I love you, and no, I will *not* read this to you at bedtime.

And finally, I'm grateful to a gloriously misspent youth crammed full of fairy tales, Disney films, and queer-coded villains. This book could never have been what it is without that.

About the Author

AIMEE OGDEN is an exciting emerging author with more than two dozen short story publications in venues such as *Analog, Shimmer, Orson Scott Card's Intergalactic Medicine Show,* and *The Dark.* Aimee is a former science teacher and software tester; she now writes stories about sad astronauts, angry princesses, and dead gods. She's also the coeditor of *Translunar Travelers Lounge,* a new speculative fiction devoted to fun, optimistic stories. She lives in Madison.

TOR·COM

**Science fiction. Fantasy. The universe.
And related subjects.**

*

More than just a publisher's website, *Tor.com*
is a venue for **original fiction, comics,** and
discussion of the entire field of SF and fantasy,
in all media and from all sources. Visit our site
today—and join the conversation yourself.